July's menu
BARONESSA GELATERIA
in Boston's North End

In addition to our regular flavors of
gelato, this month we are featuring:

- **A pool of sinful melted chocolate**

  Dark-haired, dark-eyed Joe Barone was
  always the gentleman, always in control. But
  Holly went to his head faster than 90-proof
  whiskey. When the heat of his desire finally
  melted away the family breeding, in its place
  he was all primal male....

- **Handmade miniature pastries**

  In the bakery Holly made masterpieces out
  of the tiniest desserts. But her safe little life
  was turned upside down by one meeting
  with the worldly, wealthy Joe Barone.

- **Red-hots**

  As if drawn by fate, Joe and Holly were
  powerless to resist their attraction. Neither
  one could cool down the fire burning deep
  inside, not when the flames had been
  dormant so long. Now they could be
  satisfied by nothing less than absolute,
  total possession.

  Buon appetito!

Dear Reader,

Experience passion and power in six brand-new, provocative titles from Silhouette Desire this July!

Begin with *Scenes of Passion* (#1519) by *New York Times* bestselling author Suzanne Brockmann. In this scintillating love story, a pretend marriage turned all too real reveals the torrid emotions and secrets of a former bad-boy millionaire and his prim heiress.

DYNASTIES: THE BARONES continues in July with *Cinderella's Millionaire* (#1520) by Katherine Garbera, in which a pretty pastry cook's red-hot passion melts the defenses of a brooding Barone hero. *In Bed with the Enemy,* (#1521) by rising star Kathie DeNosky, is the second LONE STAR COUNTRY CLUB title in Desire. In this installment, a lady agent and her lone-wolf counterpart bump more than heads during an investigation into a gun-smuggling ring.

What would you do if you were *Expecting the Cowboy's Baby* (#1522)? Discover how a plain-Jane bookkeeper deals with this dilemma in this steamy love story, the second Silhouette Desire title by popular Harlequin Historicals author Charlene Sands. Then see how a brokenhearted rancher struggles to forgive the woman who betrayed him, in *Cherokee Dad* (#1523) by Sheri WhiteFeather. And in *The Gentrys: Cal* (#1524) by Linda Conrad, a wounded stock-car driver finds healing love in the arms of a sexy, mysterious nurse, and the Gentry siblings at last learn the truth about their parents' disappearance.

Beat the summer heat with these six new love stories from Silhouette Desire.

Enjoy!

Melissa Jeglinski
Senior Editor, Silhouette Desire

Please address questions and book requests to:
Silhouette Reader Service
U.S.: 3010 Walden Ave., P.O. Box 1325, Buffalo, NY 14269
Canadian: P.O. Box 609, Fort Erie, Ont. L2A 5X3

Cinderella's Millionaire

KATHERINE GARBERA

Published by Silhouette Books
America's Publisher of Contemporary Romance

To my Italian family, for making me proud of where we came from
and challenging me to go in new directions. Especially my uncle, Pat Nappi,
for showing me the beauty inside, and my mom, Charlotte Smith,
for showing me how to carry on our traditions.

Acknowledgments:

Thanks to Eve Gaddy for taking time from her busy schedule
to help critique. I'm so glad fate put us in each other's paths
and made us friends!

Special thanks and acknowledgment are given to Katherine Garbera
for her contribution to the DYNASTIES: THE BARONES series.

 SILHOUETTE BOOKS

ISBN 0-373-76520-7

CINDERELLA'S MILLIONAIRE

Books by Katherine Garbera

Silhouette Desire

The Bachelor Next Door #1104
Miranda's Outlaw #1169
Her Baby's Father #1289
Overnight Cinderella #1348
Baby at His Door #1367
Some Kind of Incredible #1395
The Tycoon's Temptation #1414
The Tycoon's Lady #1464
Cinderella's Convenient Husband #1466
Tycoon for Auction #1504
Cinderella's Millionaire #1520

KATHERINE GARBERA

comes from a large Italian family. Being part of the
Barones gave her a chance to once again visit with char-
acters who share her background. She lives in the sub-
urbs of Chicago with her husband and their two children.
Writing romance is a dream come true for the author
who says that happy endings should be a part of everyone's life.

DYNASTIES:
THE
BARONES

Meet the Barones of Boston—
An elite clan caught in a web of danger,
deceit…and desire!

Who's Who in
CINDERELLA'S MILLIONAIRE

Joe Barone—He's the practical, aloof one of the
multimillion-dollar Barone clan. A widower for five years,
he's had his heart on ice for so long, he fears it's forever
frozen. Until he meets a woman who dares to melt it…

Holly Fitzgerald—For this hardworking pastry chef, life
is all about responsibilities—to her job, to her father and
brothers who need her. Until she meets Joe and finds *need*
replaced by *desire*…

Gina Barone Kingman—A PR maven, she knows what
people want even before they do. And she can see it
clearly in her brother's eyes….

One

There were times when it didn't pay to be a part of a big Italian family, Joseph Barone thought as he listened to his sister Gina give him last-minute instructions on how to handle the press today. She was the VP of PR, and in his opinion the one who should be escorting the contest winner—Holly Fitzgerald—around. But Gina and her husband, Flint, a noted spin doctor, thought it would be better if a top executive did the honors. And somehow he—the CFO—was the only one who could get up at five in the morning to handle this latest volley in Baronessa's PR plan.

"If anyone brings up the passion fruit gelato debacle, acknowledge that it was a mistake and one that Baronessa won't make again. Then use the fact sheet I gave you on the new flavor."

"Got it," he said.

Gina smiled at him. "Thanks for doing this."

"As if I had any choice." Joe had tried arguing but it was hard to win with his mother or sisters. Italian women never fought fair, and in the end, guilt and familial duty had won out.

"Mom thought you'd be the best one."

"Yeah, once you convinced her of it. You owe me, Gina."

She ignored his remark and consulted the schedule in her hand. "I'm going to check and see if the contest winner is here yet."

Joe watched his sister walk away. Gina was tall compared to other women, but she'd always be his little sister. She had changed in the last few months since her marriage to Flint Kingman. She now wore her curly light brown hair down instead of pinning it up. But then, finding the love of your life could do that to a person. She radiated a glow that only a woman in love had, and he was a little scared to see her so much in love with her new husband.

He'd changed after he'd met Mary. And then changed again after she'd died. But some things were better left in the past—and Mary was one of them.

Though it was only a little after seven, he knew his entire day was shot. He resigned himself to working half the night to make sure the forecasts they'd done for this new gelato flavor were correct. Baronessa needed a shot in the arm, and this contest, as harebrained as he'd thought it was at first, might be the answer.

He sat in one of the first-floor conference rooms in the five-story building that housed the executive offices, patiently having makeup put on for the television interviews he was doing this morning. He had an inkling of why neither his dad, the CEO, or brother Nicholas, the COO, had been unable to free their schedule today.

But Baronessa was worth a few sacrifices and certainly worth the ribbing he'd have to endure if any of his siblings wandered in while he was in the makeup chair.

To distract himself, he glanced around the room. A sense of well-being assailed him as it always did when he realized he was a part of something that had grown from a small family business into an international company. There was something about knowing exactly where you came from.

And there was something about being surrounded by his family history every day that soothed his wounded heart. Most of the time.

The gelateria had grown into more than an ice-cream shop founded in the forties by his grandparents Marco and Angelica and was now a Fortune 500 company. One Joe was proud to work for. He loved his job as CFO and had cut his teeth working for a large entertainment company in California before coming back to Boston and taking his place in the family business.

"Here she is," Gina said, entering the conference room with another woman.

Joe's breath caught in his chest. The woman walking toward him bore an uncanny resemblance to his deceased wife. Slim and petite, she had auburn hair that fell in waves around her shoulders. Mary's hair had been shorter, he thought. But her features were similar. Heart-shaped face, full lips and a nose that curved the slightest bit to the right at the end.

Joe prided himself on his resilience. He'd survived things that would have destroyed a lesser man. But he didn't want to tour the company's headquarters with the doppelgänger of his deceased wife. Gina would just have to do it.

"Holly Fitzgerald, this is my brother and Baronessa's chief financial officer, Joseph Barone."

"Pleased to meet you, Ms. Fitzgerald," Joe said, shaking her hand. Her hand in his felt soft, small, fragile. Damn. It had been a long time—five years to be exact—since he'd held a hand that delicate.

"Please call me Holly."

He nodded. He'd survived by keeping himself aloof from women, by letting no one but family close to him, and he didn't intend to let this contest winner rock the secure moorings of his world. "Gina, can I speak to you privately for a minute?"

"Of course. Holly, why don't you see our makeup artist. There's coffee, tea and juice on the sideboard. We'll be right back."

Joe didn't wait for his sister but walked out of the

conference room. His brother-in-law was tall with chocolate brown hair and, according to his sisters, drop-dead gorgeous.

"Where's Holly?" Flint asked as soon as Joe stepped into the hallway.

"In makeup."

"Damn. How long do you think it'll take?" Flint asked.

"I don't know. Go check on her."

"I will. Joe, don't go anywhere. The satellite uplink is ready and we have about ten minutes before the first interview."

Gina came out of the room and the look on her face let him know she wasn't pleased with him. "What's up?"

"I can't do this," Joe said.

"Joe, we've been over this. There is no one else," Gina said.

When Gina talked to him like that, he felt like a four-year-old who wasn't getting his way. But there was not a chance he was going to spend the day with a woman who reminded him of things he didn't want to remember.

"Okay, she's almost ready," Flint said, coming back out.

"He isn't," Gina said, pointing at her brother.

"We don't have time for this," Flint said. "You both have to be out in the garden now so that we can get on the morning-news segments on the East Coast."

Gina tried reassuring him again. "Joe, you'll do fine. Stick with the script I gave you."

"I'm not nervous about the interview. I just don't want to spend the day with her."

"Joe—"

"I don't want to spend the day with him, either," Holly said from the doorway. "In fact, I just want my check and then I'll be happy to go."

Of course, he didn't want to spend the day with her, Holly thought. She probably looked as if she spent too much time in the kitchen, which of course she did. In fact, this morning she'd gotten to the bakery at 3:00 a.m. because of her obligation to Mrs. Kirkpatrick, the owner of the small downtown bakery where Holly worked.

She felt out of place in this old-money office building and wanted nothing more than to get back into her chef's uniform and back into her pastry kitchen.

She hated the spotlight. She wouldn't have entered the Baronessa contest except for the thousand-dollar prize. She needed that money to pay her father's hospital bills. HMOs had pretty much alienated small businessmen from affordable health care, and her mechanic father was no exception.

But that didn't explain why Joseph Barone wanted nothing to do with her. He was attractive in a way that made her uncomfortable. She'd grown up around men, having helped to raise her three brothers, but something about this Barone made everything feminine in her spring to life.

He watched her the way a panther watches prey. Not afraid of her, exactly, but ready to pounce if she did anything threatening. Was he afraid she'd embarrass Baronessa?

Damn. She should have checked her appearance in the mirror before she'd come in. Maybe she still had flour on her face or in her hair.

Gina Barone-Kingman took her arm. "Holly, we can't do that. Baronessa needs the publicity your gelato will bring."

"I'm willing to do my part," Holly said. And she was. She'd never shrunk from her responsibilities and didn't intend to now. Even if there was something she couldn't identify in Joseph's eyes....

"Listen, Gina, we need to talk," Joseph said, stepping forward.

Flint Kingman took control. "Not now."

Holly had met the man earlier. She could tell he worked in public relations by the way he moved and talked. He had a quick smile and a confident, take-charge attitude. She liked him, but had the feeling he could charm just about anyone.

"Outside, both of you," Flint ordered.

Flint took Joe's arm and herded them all out the front doors into a beautiful garden awash with colorful flowers. A camera crew stood ready, while the makeup team put some finishing touches on Holly.

Suddenly she didn't know if she was going to be

able to talk intelligently with a camera on her. She'd never really been proficient at public speaking. She'd made it her practice to blend into the background, and she was very good at it.

"Until I arrived this morning, I didn't know we were doing television interviews," she said softly.

"Relax, you'll do just fine," Flint said, patting her shoulder. His touch and tone made her believe his words.

Although he was kind, he was steely in his determination. She made a note to read the fine print before entering another contest. In fact, the only thing she hated more than speaking in public was seeing herself speaking in public. She only hoped none of the Boston stations would pick up this satellite feed and use it.

Flint gestured for her and Joe to sit in some director's chairs that were set up in front of a screen with the Baronessa logo on it. Holly's hands shook so badly that she had to clench them together.

Joseph reached over and covered her hands with his. His touch surprised her. She glanced up to see if his expression had changed, but his eyes were still guarded. His hand on hers was big and warm, his nails neatly manicured. Not at all like the masculine hands she was used to seeing. Hands with dirt under the nails and calluses on their palms.

"Don't worry. I might not like this but I know what I'm doing," Joseph said.

"That's reassuring." She meant it. She needed his

experience to navigate this. She'd have to make sure to someday return the favor.

He removed his hand. "I thought it might be."

Around them stage techs bustled, making adjustments to mikes and cameras. Flint and Gina both gave them last-minute tips, and then everyone backed away. Through it all, Holly wondered why Joseph didn't want to spend the day with her. If it were the press, she could understand. She too, was reluctant to be interviewed all day long.

But it couldn't be, because he said he knew how to handle them. It must be her. This was a new record for Holly. She'd never had a man detest her on sight before.

"Can I ask you something, Joseph?"

"Sure, and call me Joe."

"Why don't you want to spend the day with me?" she asked. She knew she shouldn't voice the question, but couldn't help herself.

Maybe she hadn't gotten enough sleep the night before. Maybe the closer you got to thirty the less control you had over your mouth. Maybe…maybe she just needed to feel as if she was sitting by a friend in the glare of the spotlight, instead of next to a man who didn't want her near him.

"It isn't anything personal."

Let it go, Hol. Just smile at the camera, talk about cooking, collect your check and get out of here.

"It kind of sounded like it," she said. What was

her deal today? Definitely not enough sleep, she decided.

Joe shrugged. "You remind me of someone."

Though he didn't say it was a woman, she sensed it was. She knew men. Knew the way they thought and acted.

So she should have known better than to ask the question that was on the tip of her tongue. Her dad and brothers would never admit a woman had broken their hearts. "Did she break your heart?"

Joe stared at her in a way that made her feel like she had a spotlight shining on her.

"Sorry, that was way too personal," Holly said quickly. But she knew by his reaction that she'd struck a chord, and she wanted to know more.

"Yes, it was." The look he gave her made her squirm in her chair. Not in embarrassment, though. It was a male look that made her blood flow a little faster. This man had a presence of sophistication that made her feel like an inexperienced prep-chef in the kitchen of a world-renowned master.

She looked around but couldn't stand the suspense. "Well, are you going to answer?"

He laughed and the sound surprised her. It was a warm sound from a very cold-looking man. A man she sensed didn't find much humor in life.

"No."

Fair enough, she thought. The stage director came over and gave them some directions, and when he left, Holly glanced over at Joe. He didn't look nervous, but she was.

"Is it my hair?" she asked after a few minutes. Men had some strange illusions about redheads.

"Is what your hair?" he asked.

"The thing that reminds you of the other person."

"Yes."

"She's not Orphan Annie, is she? Because I thought all the makeup I'm wearing covered my freckles."

He didn't smile but she sensed his amusement. "No."

"No to freckles or to Annie?"

"Annie. I can still see your freckles."

"I knew it. I'm covered with them."

"Everywhere?" he asked in an intimate voice.

"Yes," she said, meeting his clear brown eyes. There was something sensual in his gaze and she couldn't look away.

Joe Barone was more than she'd expected him to be and that unnerved her. She felt safe flirting with him, for some reason. Well, safe wasn't really how she felt, but it was fun. It was weird to realize she didn't understand him—he didn't fit with what she'd come to expect from men—and even stranger to realize that she wanted to.

Her freckles weren't the only things about Holly Fitzgerald that lingered in his mind. Her sweet scent lingered on the air—something homey that reminded him of his mom's kitchen at the holidays and something else more elusive. An aroma distinct to Holly and no other woman.

She's in your life for a day, he told himself. He'd best ignore it.

But he couldn't. His groin was tight and his blood ran heavy whenever he thought about those damn freckles on her creamy skin. He wanted to strip that professional-looking suit from her body and find each and every freckle. To caress it first with his fingers, then with his tongue.

Whoa, boy. Obviously it was past time to start dating again. But he'd never been into casual sex. Even before Mary, he'd slept with only two other women and no one since her death five years ago. He'd completely shut off that part of his nature— until today when it roared back to life, demanding his attention.

The stage techs broke down the equipment, and the garden was slowly returning to its beauty. This place had long been one of Joe's favorites. He'd found solace here more than once, but not today.

The July sun beat down on him, but that wasn't the source of the heat running through his veins. No, a certain redhead was responsible. "No redheads" had been more of a safety precaution than a rule. Still, he knew better.

Why wasn't his body getting the message?

Holly laughed at something his sister said, and his groin tingled to life. He needed to get away, but for once his pager was silent. Giving in to the pull he felt from her, he joined her and Gina at the coffee and pastry table.

"So, are you over your fit?" his sister asked.

Only family treated him as if he was a defanged tiger. Everyone else in his world trod lightly around him, treating him like a loose cannon. He wished he understood why because then maybe he could wield that cannon against his sister. "Gina, I'm trying to remember why I tolerate you."

"Familial duty." Gina smiled up at him.

"Right now I wouldn't mind being disinherited."

Gina laughed. "Joe, you know we're Italian. There's no escaping the family."

He smiled at his sister. He knew she always had Baronessa's success at heart and that she'd worked hard to prove herself to the family. "Sorry I tried to back out."

"Hey, it's okay. Flint's ideas are always bigger than he makes them out to be."

Gina left to join her husband, and an awkward silence fell between him and Holly. Joe wasn't an open and gregarious man. Never really had been. But the past few years he'd fallen deeper and deeper into a silence he found comforting.

Holly lifted her hair off the back of her neck as the sun rose in the sky. She had to be hot in that suit she wore. A few tendrils of curling red hair clung to her nape. The skin there was covered with those freckles she seemed worried about. He took a sip from the Evian bottle in his hand to keep from leaning down and blowing on her overheated skin.

"So..." she said.

He raised one eyebrow at her. If she had an inkling of the direction his thoughts had been heading, he was in deep water.

"Are you ready to confess all?" she asked with a gamine grin.

"No. But I am curious about you." Joe decided to go on the offensive and drive her back into hiding. He'd been called brooding more than once by the women he'd dated. Why was it so hard to keep Holly at arm's length?

"I'm an open book," she said.

Her blue eyes said otherwise. *Interesting*. He'd really like to delve beneath her depths and uncover her secrets. But he didn't think he could do that and still keep her at arm's length.

"Yes. I already know you're a pastry chef," he said.

She took a bottle of water from the refreshment table. "In fact, I was at work this morning before I came down here."

"You must really love baking," he said. Though his family had made its name in the gelato business, Joe had never taken to baking or cooking. He could heat frozen dinners and reheat the casseroles that his mom sometimes sent to her kids' houses. But beyond that he wasn't even interested in trying.

She put the water down and stepped closer to him.

Again her scent assailed him. It was time to end this conversation and get on with the rest of the day's activities. As soon as she answered, he'd say something vague and move away from her.

"I do. The kitchen is the only place where I'm totally in control. Totally alone. There's a…peace to it."

"Why aren't you ever alone?" he asked.

"Family," she said. That one word summed up the way he sometimes felt about his.

He patted her shoulder trying for a brotherly touch, but knew he failed. Her arm under his hand was soft and he couldn't help sliding his hand down to her tiny wrist. She wore a charm bracelet there with a tiny gold rolling pin on it. "I know what you mean."

Who had given her the bracelet? A lover? Jealousy took him by surprise and he ran his finger under the fine gold chain, resting his finger on her pulse. It threaded steadily.

"Joe?"

Ah, hell, he thought. He knew better. Why was he even looking at her this way? "Did a man give you this?"

"Yes," she said huskily.

"A lover?"

Her pulse doubled. "No."

Her pupils had dilated and he saw more than awareness in them. He saw the same hunger that was coursing through his veins. Her lips parted and the air around them seemed to stop moving.

He leaned forward. "Would anyone object if I kissed you?"

"Are you going to kiss me?" she asked.

"Yes."

"There's no man in my life," she said. Holly watched him with feminine speculation in her eyes, and Joe knew he'd never be the same.

Two

Joe lifted her wrist slowly. Her heart beat so hard she thought it would jump out of her chest. Sensation trembled through her body, but she was helpless to stop it.

His breath brushed against her wrist, warming the gold chain her dad had given to her for her twenty-first birthday. Though Joe's mouth didn't touch her, she felt the humid warmth, and a sensual beating started deep in her center.

Holly's experience with men outside her family had been limited. She'd worked during high school, which had left her little time to date. Then she'd skipped college and went instead to the Culinary Institute.

But that didn't explain why she hadn't dated in the past six months. The truth was, few guys wanted to wait for her to finish working two shifts at the bakery, and drive to her dad's house to fix dinner for him and her brothers before getting to her place to get ready for a date. The men she had dated tended to be career-minded as she was, and ultimately more interested in their jobs than in her. None of them had had a tenth of the raw sexuality she sensed in Joe Barone.

His dark eyes blazed with a passion she'd read about but never experienced. His mouth on her inner wrist started a chain reaction that ended deep inside her. His hand on her arm forced her to remember she was more than a sister and chef.

Joe reminded her that she was a woman in every sense of the word. He called to her femininity and made her want to reach under the civilized facade and bring the elemental man to the surface. A man she sensed needed more than the solace he could find in her body.

Instincts she'd spent years ignoring forced her to take notice. Damn, she wasn't sure she wanted him to wake her up now. There wasn't time in her life for a man. Sure, this could be a little harmless flirting, but it felt like more.

She curled her fingers around his jaw. He was clean-shaven but she felt the fine stubble under her fingers. He turned his head in her palm and dropped one kiss in the center of it.

He nipped the fleshy part of her hand before lifting his head. He looked up into her eyes and she felt the world drop away. She wasn't aware of where she was or what she was doing. She only knew that she wanted to bask in the intensity of his gaze for a long time.

Standing on tiptoe, she brought her face closer to his. His scent was spicy and outdoorsy. She shut her eyes and inhaled deeply, then leaned just the tiniest bit toward him.

His suit and hers should have provided a better barrier but didn't. His heat and strength still surrounded her. His grip on her wrist changed and his hand slid around her waist, resting on the small of her back.

"Holly?" His voice was husky and deep.

She opened her eyes.

"I want more."

She shivered, afraid to ask for what she wanted. But she'd always lived by the rule that honesty was the best policy. "Me too."

"This could be complicated," he said.

"It doesn't have to be," she said. She'd learned enough about life to know that you took what you wanted when it was offered because it seldom was presented to you again.

"I thought you were going to kiss me," she said.

"I was."

"Changed your mind?"

He shook his head.

"Then what?"

"We need privacy for the kind of kiss I want to give you."

Holly forgot all about everything at his words. He'd shocked her. Not what he'd said but that she'd inspired it. She wasn't really a lust-at-first-sight kind of girl. But he made her feel like one.

"Mr. Barone?" a woman called from the open doorway.

"Yes, Stella," Joe said, turning toward the woman but not letting go of Holly.

Holly stood there watching him. The sound of his deep voice rushed over her. She didn't listen to his words, just wondered what it would be like to curl up next to him in bed, her head resting on his shoulder while he murmured words in that baritone voice of his.

"I'll meet you in the foyer for your building tour in ten minutes," he said to Holly.

"What?" she asked.

"Stella needs me to sign a few papers upstairs," he said.

"Oh. I wasn't listening," she said.

"What were you doing?" he asked, that teasing note back in his voice.

"Dreaming," she said, which was the truth. Reality was that this man would probably never be in her bed letting her rest on his shoulder no matter how much passion was between them. Because that dream was one she'd sought for a long time and had never found. No matter whose shoulder she'd lain on, it had never made her feel safe the way she'd imagined it would.

"Dreaming about what?"

"Being someplace more private," she said, then stepped away from him.

"Damn, if it wasn't for my family, I'd sweep you off to my place."

Ditto, she thought. Family obligations kept them both here when they'd rather be elsewhere. But Holly knew deep in her soul that family obligations would also keep them apart.

"Go do your business, Joe."

"This conversation isn't over."

"It would be better if it was," she said.

"Do you always do what's best?" he asked.

"Don't you?"

"You'll have to try me and see," he said, then pivoted and walked away.

Joe Barone was too sexy by half. A long time ago she'd promised herself that she'd live each moment to the fullest. For the first time she trod lightly on that vow because something in Joe made her doubt she could protect herself and remember her own rule. The rule that was more a vow she'd made to protect her heart from loss: Men were off-limits because she had her family to take care of.

Joe couldn't believe how fast the day had gone. The day that had promised to be endless was flying by. Already they'd toured the warehouse, done a lunchtime give-away of Holly's winning gelato at Faneuil Hall and granted interviews to the print media. The YMCA kids' summer day camp was their second-to-last stop.

Holly looked cute with her apron and chef's hat on. Too cute. He'd tried to retreat behind his wall of silence, but she'd seemed to sense what he was doing and hadn't let him. She'd kept the conversation going all day and he'd realized he liked the person Holly was. She was a hard worker, which didn't surprise him. Her days were as long as his, and her family loyalty couldn't be questioned. She'd taken three calls from her brothers on her cell phone at various points during the day.

He thought more about what he had to offer a woman and realized that he didn't want to hurt Holly. At best he could give her one night. That was all he had in him. All he'd allow himself to indulge in. And she deserved more.

He forced his thoughts back to the present. The kids at the day camp all got a kick out of asking her questions about baking. She was better with the kids than she'd been with the media.

"How did you come up with the winning flavor?" one of the teachers asked.

The reporters had asked Holly many times over, but still he was interested in hearing about how she'd devised Heavenly Berry.

"I just experimented with different combinations

of fruit and chocolate until I found one I liked. Then I gave it to my harshest critics,'' she said.

"What's a critic?" asked a little girl in ponytails. He didn't know many kids, so he wasn't sure of her age, but she looked to be maybe five. Holly put her ice-cream scoop down and knelt in front of the child.

"Someone who gives you his opinion on something you've done.''

"Like a teacher?" the little girl asked.

"Kind of. In this case it was my brothers.''

"My brothers never like anything I do,'' the girl said.

Holly brushed her hand over the child's head. She wasn't shy about touching others, except for him. She hadn't touched him at all since their morning encounter. He wondered why.

"Brothers are like that. But mine are very honest about my cooking. So I welcome their comments,'' Holly said.

"What'd your brothers say?'' Joe asked. What would he have to do to get her to touch him again?

He wanted to know more about her family. Wanted to know details of her life so he could stop looking at her and seeing a feminine mystery and instead see someone whom he knew and understood. He doubted the questions would bring him that knowledge but at least they took his mind off the way her skirt pulled tight around her hips when she'd bent to talk to the child.

Holly glanced up at him. "That I'd found the right combination."

"Really?" the girl asked.

"Yes," Holly said, standing. She handed the child a cone Joe had scooped.

The line moved quickly and soon the children were gone. The empty gym felt strange with only him and Holly. Joe's mind wasn't on the sticky ice cream on his fingers but on the smudge of gelato on Holly's cheek.

Ignore it, he advised himself, but he knew he wasn't listening. He reached over and rubbed his thumb lightly over her cheek. She shivered.

Damn, it wasn't fair that life should put in front of him this woman who reacted so quickly to his touch. Because though he'd lived a solitary life for a long time, he'd never been any good at denying himself. And it had been a long time since he'd seen a woman he'd wanted as much as he wanted Holly.

"Why are you staring at me like that?" she asked as they cleaned up the gelato containers.

"Like what?" he asked, removing his apron and folding it with exaggerated precision. Somehow he couldn't look into those clear blue eyes of hers for another minute without taking the kiss he'd wanted all day.

"Like you're wondering if I'll taste as good as the gelato," she said.

"Because that's what I'm thinking," he said, taking a step toward her. He should be backing away but he was tired of living his life in solitary confinement. Even if he'd placed himself there. Holly reminded him what he was missing, and for this one day he wanted to wallow in it.

"Dangerous thoughts, Barone," she said, knitting her fingers together.

"I know, Fitzgerald." He wished he could banter with Holly the way he did with Gina, but he'd never once had the white-hot burning desire to kiss his sister.

A long minute passed and he knew he should just grab his suit jacket and walk out the door. Gina and Flint had already left to go ahead and get the press ready for the check presentation.

But he also knew Holly awakened something deep inside him that he couldn't silence. "You're a very touchy person."

"Easily offended?" she asked.

"No, demonstrative. You've touched Flint's arm every time you talk to him and Gina's, as well," he said.

"It's part of how I communicate."

"Why haven't you touched me?"

Stark silence followed his question. He heard a car horn outside and the kids laughing on the playground. Even the sound of Holly's breathing seemed loud.

"I hadn't noticed I wasn't."

He knew the fine art of evasion when he saw it, and Holly Fitzgerald was doing her best to tap-dance out of his reach. He should let her go. Would if he had a lick of sense. But for some reason sense had deserted him. His body said he wouldn't miss it. But experience promised he would. "I did."

She shrugged. She tilted her head to one side and nibbled at that full lower lip of hers. "I'm not myself around you."

"How's that?" he asked.

She shook her head and looked away. "I can't explain it."

"Can't or won't?"

She glanced back and shrugged again. Why was she running scared? What had he done that had made her put up her shields and hide?

"All right, won't," she admitted.

She removed her chef's hat and apron and picked up her purse. "If memory serves, our last stop is at the gelateria."

"Yes," he said.

"I'll meet you there," she said, pivoting on her heel.

"Holly?"

She glanced back at him, her red hair reflecting the late-afternoon sun that streamed in through the high windows.

"I don't want you to be uncomfortable," he said.

"I know. It's not a bad thing. It's just that…" She walked back to him. "You make me feel too much, and I'm not sure how to handle it." She reached up and brushed her fingers against his jaw. "Does this make you feel better?"

"In a hundred ways," he said.

"But we have someplace to be," she said.

He nodded. She turned again and this time he let her go. He watched the sway of her hips with each step she took. He watched her leaving and knew deep in his soul that he should remember this picture of her. That he shouldn't let himself get involved because she wasn't going to stay in his life.

Holly had never been in the flagship Baronessa Gelateria. She had a pint of Baronessa's Rocky Guava in her freezer at home. It was the one constant in her kitchen aside from cooking and baking staples.

Gina and Flint had the press stationed in one area and a few customers at the tables. Off to the side was a group of people clustered together. There had to be at least twenty-five of them looking on.

In came Joe. He had his suit jacket on and looked polished and professional. Holly wondered if that was the barrier he used to keep people at a distance.

She was relieved the day was over but she wished she'd had more time with Joe. Alone time.

But that was something she'd be better off without. He made her feel that human spontaneous combustion might be possible. He made her want things that she was used to living without. He made her ache with the knowledge that who she was and who she wanted to be still weren't the same person.

She sighed.

"Hang in there. We're almost through," Joe said.

She smiled up at him. The drive to the gelateria had been in rush-hour traffic, which had been good. It had forced her mind off of this disturbing man.

But here he was filling the crowded room and making her want things she knew better than to ask for. The press had been trying, but his company had made it a nice day. Tonight when she went home she'd dream of him and what might have been.

"It has been a long day," she said. Great, she'd gone from flirting to inane. He'd knocked her off balance and she was having a hard time finding her footing.

He reached for her and then dropped his hand, cursing under his breath.

"What's the matter?" she asked.

She didn't understand why but she needed to know more about him. To probe those depths that he kept hidden. Though he'd been flirtatious and teasing with her most of the day, he'd protected himself carefully from her. She knew there was more to him than his civilized exterior showed her.

He was a tall, dark and brooding man who watched her with that keen sexual desire that made her ultra-aware of him. Yet he didn't want to give her anything but the sexual awareness. She didn't have to be a genius to figure that out. The part she didn't understand was if it was only her or all women that he reacted to in that way.

He rubbed his jaw where a faint five o'clock shadow could be seen making him look rougher than he had earlier. It was as if the real man under the facade was starting to come to the surface. Her palms tingled and she wanted to cup his face in her hands and feel the roughness of his skin against hers.

"My family is here," he said at last, nodding toward the large group she'd noticed earlier.

"How many siblings do you have?"

"Three brothers and four sisters, plus four cousins. It looks like most of them decided to put in an appearance."

"And that's bad?" she asked. She'd be flattered if her father and brothers ever showed up at something she did.

"Hell, yes," he said.

"I think it's sweet."

"Really?"

"Yes."

"Why?"

She should have kept her mouth shut because there was no way to tell him why without revealing her vulnerability. She could only hope he wouldn't notice. "Because it shows how much they care about you."

He flushed at little. "Well, it might not mean that. This is a big Baronessa deal, and my dad is the CEO and Nick is the COO. So technically they have to be here."

Holly glanced again at the group of Joe's family.

They were a city unto themselves, talking and laughing. And he had sisters. And maybe sisters-in-law. She'd always wanted a sister. And she envied him not only the support of his family but also his sisters.

"Why is it so hard to believe they'd want to be here for you?" she asked.

"It's not. Except the last few years I haven't been the easiest person to get along with."

"You?" she asked, surprised.

"You don't think so."

"You've been… I'm afraid to say it in case you take it the wrong way."

"You'll have to take your chances," he said, moving closer to her. Barely an inch of space separated them.

"I'm not a risk taker," she admitted, taking a half step back.

"I am," he said, and the words seemed to surprise him.

She didn't want to be the only one revealing a weakness. Why didn't she just make something up? She didn't have to tell him that he reminded her of a fairy-tale prince. A white knight on a charger who'd ride to her rescue. She didn't have to say the words out loud. Wouldn't have to hear them and cringe. Wouldn't have to acknowledge that he awakened dreams she'd buried deep and hoped to forget about for the rest of her life.

"If I tell you, you owe me an explanation about who I remind you of."

"Stop stalling," he said.

She glanced up at him and found him waiting patiently.

"You have been my white knight today," she said softly.

Before he could speak, Gina came over. "Okay, you two, this is it. Joe, you'll present the check. Holly, you'll accept it. Then you're free to go."

Holly followed Gina to the front of the store, while Joe stood there. She knew he wanted to say something to her. Maybe it was for the best that he hadn't. That way she could keep him hidden in her memory as a dream of what could have been.

Three

Holly placed the check from Baronessa carefully in her wallet. Joe's family had been a little intimidating, almost more than the press, but now everything was over. She could return to being regular old Holly.

Tomorrow morning she'd be back in the bakery and Joe would be back to his life. She'd miss the feminine excitement that Joe had sparked, but apparently fate had given them only this one day.

She hadn't even had a chance to try her winning flavor, which the Barones had decided to call Heavenly Berry. Holly was impressed with Baronessa's savvy marketing and PR team. It was easy to see why they were the number one gelato company in the U.S.

She adjusted the strap on her purse and headed toward the door. Leaving without saying goodbye to Joe seemed weird to her, but, then, saying goodbye would be awkward.

She wondered if she could get to the bank before the drive-up teller closed. She glanced at her watch. Not unless traffic was light.

"Got a date?" Joe asked from behind her.

She turned and noticed the crowd had dispersed.

"No. Nothing that exciting. I was trying to decide if I could make it to the bank before it closed."

His gaze met hers. She'd always thought brown eyes were kind of average, not very exciting, but something about Joe's eyes made her react. Made her think of deep pools of rich warm chocolate. She licked her lips, sure he'd be just as yummy as the decadent dessert.

"What did you decide?" he asked.

"That the chances are slim."

"Good."

"Good?" she asked. Damn, he liked to tease her and she enjoyed it. Too much, she thought, because he made her want to be reckless.

He arched one eyebrow at her. "That's what I said."

"Why?" She smiled at him.

"I hoped you'd join me for dinner."

She swallowed. "You move fast."

"I wish we could move even faster."

She didn't know why, but that line of questioning seemed even more dangerous than his touch. A couple brushed by them to be seated. "We should get out of the way."

Joe took her arm and led her outside. The late-summer evening was warm and the street traffic in the North End wasn't too bad considering the hour. The sun lay low on the horizon.

His touch made her remember all the reasons she'd enjoyed his company. And all the reasons she'd been careful not to touch him all day. She didn't want to have to feel alive in the way only he made her feel. She took a tiny step away from him, to give herself some breathing room, but he just stepped closer. Damn, he smelled good.

"About dinner," he said.

"What about it?" she asked, not trusting the excitement building inside her.

"Are you available?"

She had to choose whether she was going to take the chance of getting to know him better or return to her normal life without knowing what those lips of his felt like on hers. "Yes."

"Great. We can go to the best Italian kitchen in Boston."

"Antonio's?"

"No. My place."

"Your place? Do I look naive?"

"No, you look tempting."

"Tempting? Not bad. But I'm still not going to your place on our first date."

"Which number does it have to be?"

"I don't know. Let me check my *Dating in the New Millennium* book."

Pretending to withdraw a book from her purse, she studied the imaginary pages for a minute. "There's no firm answer. It depends on the guy."

Joe scooted even closer to her and she closed her eyes, afraid he'd see that she wasn't the sophisticated, witty woman she'd been pretending to be.

"What are you looking for, Holly?"

"Tonight?"

He nodded.

"A nice dinner with a good-looking Italian."

"I can get you the nice dinner. Would a surly Italian do?"

"I have yet to see surly but if he shows up, we'll renegotiate."

"Deal."

"There's a nice quiet little deli around the corner. Does that sound good?"

"Yes," she said. They walked next to each other. His heat enveloped her and she wished she'd worn a blouse under her suit jacket so she could take it off and feel his touch on her skin.

"Do you have big plans for your money?" he asked.

"Yes."

"What are you buying?"

She just shook her head. She didn't want to talk about her father and his health problems.

"My sisters would spend it on clothes or shoes."

"I'd love to spend it on shoes," Holly said. In fact, she'd had her eye on a pair of strappy sandals since spring, but she didn't really need them since she spent most of her time at the bakery or home.

"What is it with women and shoes?" he asked, but there was a teasing note in his voice.

His gaze skimmed down her legs, stopping at the Enzo pumps she'd bought on sale last summer. "Those look nice, by the way."

"My legs or shoes?"

"Your legs," he said.

"Thanks. I'd return the compliment but I haven't seen yours yet."

He laughed and it made her feel good deep inside. She wanted this day to never end. She thought maybe she'd been too hasty in telling him she couldn't go to his place tonight, because suddenly she wanted to—very badly.

Marino's reminded him of being a kid again. Until he walked in the front door he'd forgotten that it had been five years since he'd been in there. He'd suggested the Italian deli because it made sense and he was a logical guy most of the time.

But suddenly logic had flown out the door. He remembered why he'd avoided the place. He'd met Mary here. It had been the summer before he started college. They'd met near the end-cap with the home-made Italian cookies. Mary had been from New Jer-

KATHERINE GARBERA   43

sey and missing home. Joe had brought her to his family, and the rest had been history.

The smell overwhelmed him—spicy oregano, pepperoni and garlic. They were the scents of his boyhood and brought with them dreams he'd done his best to forget. He paused in the doorway, doubts penetrating the desire that had been motivating him since he'd met Holly. What the hell was he doing?

Holly bumped into him. "Is it too crowded?" she asked.

Joe shook his head. Only in his mind was it crowded—with two women who looked the same. Actually, there was only a couple of teenage boys at one of the tables in the front and Robert behind the deli counter.

"Joseph, it's been a long time since we've seen you. Mama, come out here and see who is in the shop," Robert said in his heavily accented English.

Joe embraced the shorter older man with true fondness. Robert and Lena were a part of his past. For the first time he was cognizant that he'd quit living when Mary died. His mom had tried to tell him but he hadn't wanted to believe her.

"Robert, how's it going?"

"Today, it's good, Joseph. For you too, eh?" Robert looked right at Holly and then winked at Joe.

"Today is good," Joe said. Though he wasn't sure. Days that passed with numbing quickness were what he usually wanted. Today had gone quickly but he'd started to feel again and it was painful. Frostbite wearing off was painful.

He turned to the source of his reawakening. "Robert Marino, this is Holly Fitzgerald. Holly, this is Robert, the proprietor of the finest Italian deli in Boston."

"Nice to meet you, Miss Fitzgerald."

"Likewise," Holly said.

Lena came out of the back and let out a little shriek of joy, ran over to Joe and embraced him. Holly was watching him with a smile in her eyes, and he realized she knew he was uncomfortable and was amused because of it. He arched his eyebrows to let her know he'd get her back later.

After they ordered their sandwiches, they made their way to one of the tables in the front. Joe felt awkward. Sexual awareness he was comfortable with, but sitting at this small table in the crowded market felt too intimate to him.

He hated being irrational and exploring his emotions, so he forced his attention to the sandwich put in front of him. He'd eat dinner with Holly and then say good-night. It had been a day out of time, but he wasn't interested in getting involved with a woman again for the long term. Sex was fine but Holly made him want more, so he wasn't going to pursue her.

"This is a really nice place. It reminds me of the bakery where I work," Holly said, shifting on her seat. Her legs rubbed against his under the table. An image of them swam in his brain, and he knew he was going down.

"You work in a bakery?" he asked. Right now he couldn't remember anything except that she had incredibly long legs for a petite woman. And all those tempting freckles on her skin.

"I told you, remember?"

"Yes, you did." If his groin would stop trying to control things, maybe he'd have a chance of sounding halfway intelligent.

"The bakery is owned by a couple like the Marinos. It's really nice. We do some Italian pastries but not too many."

"You said you started baking to get away from your family?" he asked. As long as he kept her talking, he could distract himself from those long, slim legs resting in between his.

"Did it sound like that? I didn't mean it that way. I bake because it's what I know how to do and I'm good at it. My family doesn't enter the kitchen."

"Why not?" he asked.

She shrugged. "Because my brothers don't like to cook."

"Really?" She always hedged when the subject of family was brought up. He didn't know why that bothered him. Maybe because she made him feel unsteady and he wanted to rock her boat as well.

"Do you like to?" she asked.

He could grill but that didn't seem like real cooking to him. Not the way his mom or some of his sisters cooked. Not the way Mary had. "Not really. But I can get by if I have to."

"I know. That's how they are."

Holly's cell phone rang, and she glanced at the caller ID and then smiled an apology at him. "I have to answer this."

He tried to ignore her conversation but couldn't. When she disconnected her call, she stood up. Her face was pale and her hands were shaking.

"I've got to go," she said, then glanced around for her purse.

"Is everything okay?" Joe asked, standing as well.

She found her bag on the floor and slung it over her shoulder. "I don't know. My dad is having an episode. I need to go home."

"Do you want me to drive you?" he asked. He hated illness and how it made the healthy feel impotent. He sensed that Holly shouldn't be alone. He barely knew her, really, but he'd sat alone in a darkened hospital room watching his wife's life slip away and he didn't want her to have to do that for her father. Though the situation with her dad sounded different, Holly's reactions were similar to his.

"No. Thanks, but I better go alone. He might have to go to the hospital." She couldn't stop shaking, and he did the only thing he could do even though his gut shouted for him to let her walk away. He pulled her into his arms and hugged her close.

"Does your dad have a chronic condition?" Joe asked after a minute.

She pushed away from him. "Yes. I don't want to talk about it."

He understood how acting normal in an emergency was sometimes the only way to keep from breaking down. "Fine. Let me walk you back to your car."

The Holly he'd first met was back. The one who had told them all she wanted was her check. The vibrancy he'd come to expect from her was hidden away, and in its place was a mask of cool indifference that seemed wrong to him.

"That's not necessary," she said.

He'd been raised better than that. "It is to me."

They gathered the remains of their aborted dinner, and Joe shouted a goodbye to the Marinos. He knew that for his own sanity he should be glad for the premature end to the night, but he wasn't. He caught up with Holly, who walked so quickly she was almost running.

"It won't do your dad any good if you hurt yourself trying to get to him," he said quietly.

She slowed her pace a little, then stopped altogether. She wrapped her arms around her waist and stood there, comforting herself when he would have gladly offered her his shoulder. But he knew she wouldn't take it. She'd proven that minutes ago in the deli when she'd pushed him away.

"I know," she said. "It's just that I won't be able to calm down until I've seen him."

They reached Baronessa's and Holly was still agitated. She shifted her keys from one hand to the other, then dropped them. She stooped to retrieve them. He worried that if she got behind the wheel in this kind of condition, she'd have an accident.

"I really think I should drive you," Joe said.

"No." She closed her eyes and took a couple of deep breaths, and when she opened her eyes, the upset woman of only a few seconds ago was gone. "I can handle this on my own. Thanks for dinner," she said. She walked away from him, and he had no choice but to watch her go.

She'd started a fire inside him that wouldn't die, but there was more to Holly Fitzgerald than awesome legs, curvy hips and sex appeal. And that was something that he wasn't sure he wanted to get involved with.

At nine o'clock in the evening Holly left her father and youngest brother, Brian, at their father's house. Brian was in college and the only one who didn't have to be at work early in the morning, so it made sense for him to stay with their dad tonight. Holly would have done it, but her brothers had insisted she go home.

They'd teased her about her television interview from that morning. Her dad had even managed a gruff compliment about the way she'd looked and sounded.

She was wiped out. He'd taken his nitroglycerin tablets, and finally the pain had subsided. But he had a heart condition and any pain was cause for alarm by her and her brothers. Sometimes she felt her dad was living on borrowed time, even though Dr. James had assured her that her father would live to give his grandkids a hard time.

A weird melancholy settled over her as she walked to her car. The 1979 MGB had seen better days but it ran like a dream, thanks to her brothers and their weekly tune-ups. She was grateful because money had been tight for as long as she could remember and a new car was way down on her list of priorities.

She drove home noticing things she hadn't thought about in a long time. Like the summer was halfway over and this morning was the first time she'd been outside in the sun. She needed to make some decisions about her life. She knew her responsibilities to her family would always be there, but she really wanted to start enjoying herself. She was almost thirty, which was scary to think about, and the most exciting day of her life had come from winning a gelato-flavor contest.

What did that say about her?

She turned onto Hanover Street and drove slowly past Baronessa's. She still hadn't sampled the new version of her flavor. She'd bet the taste wasn't exactly the same as when she made it. When you multiplied a recipe some of the nuance of the flavor changed. She'd seen it happen once or twice with a pastry filling.

She pulled into a parking space. She'd get a sample of the new flavor and take it home. She had plans with her VCR and her favorite pajamas.

Baronessa Gelateria was doing a steady business. She scanned the tables, which were a little lighter at this time of night than the take-out line. Joe was still here. She started to glance away before he looked up but then decided not to. She wanted to see him again. Especially if the crazy beating of her pulse was any indication.

When he saw her, she waved. He waved back reluctantly. She had the feeling she was seeing the surly man he'd warned her about.

The couple he was dining with glanced around at her, and she recognized them from earlier—his parents. For what seemed an eternity they chatted with Joe, and Holly waited in line. Finally the couple in front of her left and Holly ordered. She was almost to the door when Joe's hand on her shoulder stopped her.

She'd didn't question how she knew it was him. She just accepted that her body knew his touch by instinct.

"I guess your dad must be okay," Joe said from behind her.

"Yeah, he's fine," she said.

"Do you have time to join me?" he asked.

She did but wasn't sure she wanted to. Today she'd realized she wanted to be the one to give her dad grandkids, and that meant she had to start dating guys who were looking for commitment. "I..."

"Why are you suddenly shy?" he asked.

"I'm not shy," she said. And she wasn't. It was just that he brought to life so many contradictory emotions that she didn't know how to react around him.

"Then what's the problem?"

"Driving home, I realized I'm in a different place than I was before I'd gone to see my dad," she said.

"So?" he asked. She had the feeling that he really wanted to know. Even though they'd known each other only a few short hours, there was a history between them. She thought it might be the same thing that linked victims of tragedy together. Once you'd been in an intense situation with someone, you formed a bond with him. But she wanted more than a passing bond with this man.

"I want more than a brief fling with you, Joe."

"I didn't know that's what I'd offered you."

She couldn't read him but she sensed he wasn't angry, only curious. He took her arm and led her outside the restaurant. He didn't stop until they were by an empty storefront a few doors away.

"Now, tell me what you're talking about," he said.

She wasn't sure she could, now that they were so close to each other in the dark with only the moon and faint glow of a streetlight to illuminate them. His features were stark and his eyes glowed with an intensity that told her to be careful what she said.

"I only meant that this morning I would have settled for one."

"But not now?" he asked.

"I don't know. I just feel like something is changing inside me. I think you made me realize I wanted more."

He sighed and rubbed the bridge of his nose. "Well, I'm not looking for more than a fling, Holly."

"I'm not sure what I'm looking for anymore," she said. She only knew that flirting and teasing weren't enough.

"Then I guess this is goodbye," he said.

She thought about it. The old Holly would have walked away without another word, but she was a new Holly. One who wasn't afraid to ask for what she wanted—well, kind of.

She took his hand in hers and stood on tiptoe, leaning toward him. "This is goodbye."

She brushed her mouth against his. His hands came up and cupped her face, tilting her head and taking control of the kiss. His lips on hers were warm and tempting. Time and place dropped away. She'd never been so totally under a man's possession before.

His lips, teeth, tongue all bade her to delve deeper. To learn every bit of this man who wouldn't be in her life after this day. His tongue traced the outline of her lips, and heat shot through her body. She shook with the force of the desire awakening in her.

She lifted her hand from his wrist, touched the edge of his jaw. His skin was warm and she rubbed her fingers over his cheek as his mouth consumed hers.

She canted her body into his, letting him support her—and wishing he was a different man but knowing that if he were she wouldn't want him with the same fire that was burning her soul.

Four

Joe's rational mind tried to warn him that he was making a foolish mistake, but he didn't care. He'd been asleep too long and Holly felt too good in his arms. He wanted her. He'd been too long without a woman to stem the desire for Holly.

She shifted, not grasping but clinging to him as her body succumbed to the web of desire he wove around them. A hot, humid breeze blew, fanning the flames that her tongue and mouth had ignited in him. He altered his grip on her, adjusting his hips to ease his hardness against her softness. When she melted into him, he'd have given ten years of his life to have nothing between them but her freckles instead of the frustrating layers of clothing.

He slid his hands down her back, cupping her buttocks in his hands, and held her still while he ground his hips against her. She moaned deep in her throat, a more sensuous sound than he'd expected from her.

He was so damn hard he could feel his pulse between his legs. He needed release—now. He needed her naked underneath him—now. He needed to stop—now, before he went too far.

He pulled back not out of any manly restraint, though that trait would be admirable. He pulled back because he'd crumble the carefully cultivated wall he'd built to protect himself from emotions.

She moaned a little, her hands still in his hair, holding him close.

"Why'd you stop?" she asked, her husky voice brushing over him like a velvet glove.

He wasn't about to reveal himself to her. To let her know or see that he wasn't the aloof man he pretended to be. "You said you didn't want to see my place tonight."

"Maybe I've changed my mind," she said.

Could he handle an affair with her? He wasn't sure he'd let it end after one night. The way he felt, once he had her in bed they weren't leaving for a long time. And could he walk away from that—from her?

He didn't want to know.

"You're tired and you had a scare with your dad. Tonight's not the right time," he said, leading her to her car.

She was stiff and tense under his guiding touch,

and he regretted that. Regretted that he'd had to stop the only thing that had made him feel good in a long time. For years he'd watched his siblings fall in love, watched Baronessa's go through numerous changes, watched life pass him by. Watched it, not lived it.

When had he turned into such a man?

"What is it?" she asked.

There was caring in her voice and he knew he shouldn't say anything else to her. Just get her to her car and get the hell away from her. But he couldn't walk away—not yet. She'd given him something he wasn't sure he wanted. But all the same she'd changed him and he owed her.

"Nothing," he said, leading her the rest of the way to her car. She'd left the top down and he wanted to warn her about criminals and safety but knew it wasn't his place. At best he was a man who'd kissed her, at worst nothing more than a stranger.

For the first time he wanted to be more. But how much more? He'd known for a long time that he'd never love again. And having lived with love, he knew he couldn't ask a woman to enter a relationship that had less than love to offer.

"I think I'm glimpsing the surly Joe," she said, leaning against the side of her car. She reached over and deposited her purse and carton of gelato on the front passenger seat. There was something different about her now. She seemed lighter almost and he wanted to know why.

He gave her a half grin. "Yeah, you are."

She tucked one of her long red curls behind her ear. "You still owe me an explanation of who I reminded you of."

"Now?" he asked.

She shrugged, the movement shifting her breasts against her jacket. "I doubt we'll have many other chances to talk," she said.

"Ah, hell, Holly."

She just waited. She wanted to know about Mary. The one woman he didn't want to discuss with Holly was Mary.

He'd been to a psychologist. Knew all about survivor guilt. But he didn't feel guilty he survived. He felt angry that Mary was gone. She'd made living more intense. And though he was a big guy and could stare down any danger, that emotional vulnerability was the scariest thing he'd ever experienced. And he never wanted to be in that place again.

Say it out loud, he told himself. A deceased spouse would provide an effective barrier between him and Holly. It would give him an escape hatch.

"You remind me of my wife," he said quietly.

She blanched. "You're married?"

Joe shook his head. "I was. She died a few years ago from cancer."

"I'm sorry," Holly said.

"Yeah." In his mind Joe clearly remembered the night five years ago when Mary had slipped away from him. Remembered clearly how a light inside him had extinguished. Remembered clearly how he'd vowed to never let another person affect him the way Mary had.

And staring down at the redhead in front of him, he knew he'd failed. Because even if he never saw her again, Holly Fitzgerald would live on in his dreams.

She felt inane. She couldn't think of a single thing to say to ease the pain that still lingered in his eyes. She knew what it was like to watch someone you loved waste away from something you couldn't control or make better. Sometimes the only solution was to escape. To get away from it all. And she didn't know if Joe should get away from her or from his memories.

Joe seemed so strong that it was hard to imagine him having the same weaknesses as she did. But his words and his eyes told her he did.

At six foot two he stood next to her and made her feel small and delicate. That was a strange feeling for her, because she'd always been the strong one others relied on. Maybe she could do that for Joe. Help him find his way and get back on his feet.

She ached for him. Ached to wrap him in her arms and comfort him in the age-old way of men and women. Ached to give him the most basic of human comfort.

The old Holly would have lingered on the North End street. But the new Holly was a woman on the cusp of change, and Joe Barone was a man not ready to make a commitment. She needed a man who was ready. Or at least able to acknowledge she was more to him than a good time.

She wasn't sure she could walk away, but common sense said to. This was a man who'd been badly hurt and wasn't going to risk injury again.

"I guess I'd better go," she said.

"Yeah, you should."

She opened the door to the MG and slid into the car. Looking up at him in the dim light, she noticed he looked alone, aloof. Much like the man she'd first met this morning. She knew she should drive away.

For her own best interest, leaving was the right choice. But she'd been alone too long. She knew exactly what it was like to always be on the outside.

He needed to get away, she thought again. Take time to do something that made no sense. Something that would take him outside his shell and into another world.

Her world? a voice inside her asked.

She wasn't sure that she wanted him in her world. But she had an idea. She told herself it was only because she needed to forget how frail her dad had looked, but the truth was, Joe had started a burning deep inside her that wasn't going away.

She needed to do something physical. Something to assuage that restlessness, even if only for a short while.

"Want to go for a ride?" she asked.

He seemed surprised but hesitated only a second. "Sure."

He walked around the car, moved the gelato and her purse and got inside. "What about your parents?"

"What about them?"

"Don't you need to say goodbye?"

"No."

He didn't say anything for a few miles as she drove through the darkened city. The wind in her hair made her feel free. Made her forget that the man next to her wasn't just a good-looking guy that she found attractive. Made her forget that she had to be at the bakery at five the next morning. Made her forget all the reasons she shouldn't bring Joe home with her tonight.

Why couldn't she? Not to stay the night but to play a little basketball.

He raised an eyebrow when she turned into her residential neighborhood.

"Where are you taking me?"

"To my house."

"I'm not objecting but why?"

"To burn off some energy."

"In your bed?"

"Maybe," she said.

"Maybe?"

"That's what I said."

"What's it going to take to make that a yes?"

"Beat me at a game of basketball."

His eyes skimmed her figure. He reached over, placing his hand on her thigh.

"What are you doing?" she asked.

"Trying to see if I'm being conned."

"Conned how?"

"Are you sandbagging me with this feminine suit and girly nails?"

She looked at him. "I'd never do that."

"I don't know. This thigh feels like it's seen its share of exercise."

"Would you believe I own a stationary bike?"

"I bet you don't use it."

"How'd you guess?"

"Because you enjoy being outside. The sun on your skin, the breeze in your hair. You, Holly Fitzgerald, are a very sensual woman."

She glanced over at him again. She wasn't sure what the teasing note in his voice meant. But his touch on her leg had changed. Now it was more caressing than probing. His fingers slid under the hem of her skirt, and with only the thin barrier of nylon to keep him from her flesh, his touch was more than enchanting. It was a fire that consumed her. Her foot jerked off the gas pedal and the MG stalled.

She removed his hand from her leg, ducked her head to avoid Mrs. Jeffers's nosey glance and restarted the car. Don't look at him, she told herself. Not until you have to.

She pulled into her driveway. Though silence filled the car, the night sounds surrounded them, and for a minute Holly lingered there. She wanted to let the sultry July air sink into her skin. Let the starry sky weave its promises. And let the man sitting next to her make his move.

"Am I still invited in?" he asked.

How the hell had she gotten herself into this? She needed to start thinking before acting. "For basketball."

"And later?"

"I'm still waiting to see if you can be the man your touch promised you were."

"That's asking a lot out of a little caress."

"I was afraid that'd be your answer."

Joe turned sideways in the passenger seat. "What do you want from me, Holly?"

"More than you can give," she said, knowing that she'd once again been shortchanged. Once again she'd settled for less than she deserved. She jerked her keys from the ignition and fumbled for the door. His hand on her arm stopped her from exiting.

"How do you know that?"

"Because your kiss was more profound than anything I've ever experienced," she said as she left the car then turned to look at him. "And it didn't mean a thing to you."

Joe wasn't used to hurting women's feelings. Hell, he didn't really interact with all that many women. Stella, his secretary, was efficient and always anticipated his needs. His mom and his sisters wouldn't let him wound them with words or deeds. Mary had been sickly for most of the time they'd been married.

Seeing Holly's deep-blue eyes shutter as she looked away made him feel like a bastard. The kind of bastard who had no business being alone with this kind of woman.

She was still shaky, and a real gentleman would have declined her offer of a ride. But then he'd proven time and again he wasn't a real gentleman. Why was it taking him so long to learn this lesson?

Despite money and breeding, Joe Barone had always been rough around the edges. And now Holly knew it too. She presented a sophisticated and professional facade, but there was something very soft about Holly Fitzgerald. He remembered her bending down to talk to the little girl at the YMCA and knew that she was lifetimes too soft for the man he'd become. The only man he knew how to be.

He climbed out of the little car and caught her arm before she could disappear. He didn't know what to say. He'd never been one of those suave guys who always sounded clever, like his older brother Nicholas. He'd give any amount of money right now for Nick's panache. Or Alex's charm.

But he didn't have it and never would. Life had proven that it took more than style and a smile for Joe to navigate it. He didn't mind, really. He did, however, mind hurting this woman.

"You shouldn't read so much into every man who kisses you." His own words sounded stilted to him.

He was out of his depth with her in this setting. Why had he allowed his gut to make a decision his mind knew was wrong?

She stood a few feet away from him, arms crossed over her chest. Spending the majority of his career in the corporate world had taught him to read body language. There was nothing open in her stance. She was angry and she wasn't afraid to let him see it.

She stepped closer. "I don't let a lot of men kiss me. And trust me, I won't let you do it again."

He could see the expression in her clear blue eyes. They were deep and mysterious and though he had no right, he wanted to explore those secrets. To find out what made her tick. He knew what made her mad, knew what upset her. But what made her laugh—suddenly he needed to know.

"The hell you say."

She arched one eyebrow at him and gave him a haughty look. "Don't go there, Joe."

"I'll go wherever I want, Holly. Or haven't you figured that out?"

She didn't back away, just stood there in the deepening night as if she'd hold her ground forever. And she probably would.

She wasn't going to let him bully her or ride roughshod over her. Even now when he wanted her to just back down and let the matter drop, she wouldn't. He wanted her to let him have his way and knew he was acting like a bully. But she'd come too close to him. Pushing her away was self-preservation.

Holly reminded him of his sister Gina. She fought when backed into a corner too, same as Holly.

But fighting hadn't been his original intent.

"I was trying to apologize," he told her finally.

"Well, you need practice."

"I know," he said wryly. He'd always hated admitting he was wrong. Especially to anyone other than himself.

She studied him. "Apology accepted."

"Are we still on for basketball?"

She nodded. He realized that she was dealing with more than just him. She had to still be worried about her father. He didn't blame her.

His parents were healthy, thank God, but they were getting older and Joe knew enough of life to know he wouldn't have them around forever. That was one of the reasons he tried to have dinner with them once a week.

"I didn't mean to push you."

"Then why did you?" she asked.

He didn't want to think about it. But the truth was, he didn't know how to manage a relationship with a woman without getting in over his head. He'd survived Mary's death but by cutting off all of his emotions.

"I don't have women friends," he said.

"So?"

"It's been a long time since I've been with a woman. You make me feel like I'm fifteen again."

She smiled and reached up to brush her fingers

across his cheek. The touch shot through him like an electric wire. He wasn't sure he could stay near her and not give in to the urge to make her his.

"You make me feel young again too, in a way I never was."

Let it go, he thought. But he couldn't. "Why?"

"My mom died when I was eighteen, but she was sick before that. I've always had to take care of my family."

"Your dad?"

"Yes, and my brothers. I'm not complaining. I'm just saying that you make me feel free."

He reached up and clasped her hand in his, leading her toward the house. Holly was a special woman who needed to be given more than one night of hot sex. He knew for both of their sanity he had to back off. He only hoped the physical exertion of basketball would cool the fire burning deep inside him. But doubted it would. That flame had been dormant too long.

Five

Though her life was very busy, basketball was the one thing Holly had always made time for. The basketball court was the one place where brothers didn't need to be reminded to do their homework, fathers didn't need to be reminded to take their nitroglycerin and pastries didn't have to be made. It was the one place where she could forget the familial responsibility that drove her and just be herself. Tonight, however, Joe made her remember more of herself than she wanted to.

She lived in an older residential neighborhood. Her garage was detached and behind the house. She had a backboard hung above the garage, and the driveway served as a court. She'd purchased the house only a year ago and was very house-proud. It wasn't one of those showplaces you saw in *Architectural Digest* but it was hers.

When she'd led Joe through the house to her spare bedroom for him to change into the clothing her brothers kept at her place, he seemed to crowd the small bungalow with his sheer presence. She hadn't realized how broad his shoulders were until she saw him framed in the doorway. Clearing her throat, she said, "Let's go outside."

"Ready to meet your match?"

"Honey, I was born ready."

She had a spotlight attached to the garage for these late-night games. It seemed she never made it home in time to play before sunset. She glanced at Joe again.

He had nice strong legs, and his arms and chest were a solid wall of muscle, his skin darkly tanned, and she regretted that there was too much between them now for a night of mindless sex.

They'd reached the point where going to bed would bring more complications. And her life was complex enough.

Joe looked younger in her brother's shorts and T-shirt than she'd expected. It was as if she were glimpsing the man he'd been before losing his wife. And though many of her feelings for him were unresolved, she was glad she'd invited him to her home tonight.

"Like what you see?" he asked.

She flushed a little at being caught staring at him. "Maybe."

"Maybe?" he asked, flexing his arms like a body-builder. "What about now?"

"Still only a maybe."

He took a menacing step toward her and she giggled. This playfulness was something new to her. Her life was so busy and so full of have-to's that she'd forgotten what it was like to just have fun.

She smiled. "Let's see what you got."

She passed him the ball and he dribbled toward the hoop, jumping and sinking the ball with an ease that would have done Michael Jordan proud. Now she'd have to concentrate on her game, when she wanted to loaf and ogle him. She took his pass and sank a jumper.

"Not all window dressing, huh?" she asked, remembering his comment in the car. And the hot touch of his hand on her thigh. Oh God. She was never going to be able to concentrate on anything while he was standing next to her all big and male.

"Lucky shot," he said, passing the ball back to her.

She dribbled the ball a few times, then ran to the hoop and scored again. She felt his eyes on her the entire time. Her concentration was shot but luckily the ball went into the hoop.

"Not bad," he said, patting her on the backside as she went by.

"Foul," she said when she could speak. His hand

was big and strong and she'd liked his touch. She wanted more of it, but knew better.

"Sorry," he said, but he didn't look sorry.

"You will be, buddy, if you don't watch out."

He smiled again, a slow, sensuous grin that made her blood heat and called everything feminine in her to the front. "It was an accident."

She wriggled her eyebrows at him. "I can cause accidents too."

"Bring it on," he said.

They played fast and furious and in the end he won. The glow of victory gleamed in his eyes. Holly had played her best and had more fun than she'd thought possible tonight.

"Good game," she said.

He nodded. "Next time we'll have to make a wager."

"I don't bet."

"Not the gambling type?" he asked.

"I wouldn't have pictured you for the risk-taking type," she said.

"Normally I'm not. But you bring out a different side to me, Holly."

He did the same to her, but the day had been long and her emotions had run the gamut from nerves to sexual attraction to fear for her dad and then back to sexual attraction before ending at the spot she was in now. A kind of weary curiosity.

She wanted to know more about Joe Barone. Already she knew he liked her freckles and played basketball to win. But she wanted to know what it would take to turn the desire burning in his eyes into something more. Though her mind said tonight was the only time they'd meet, her heart didn't want to believe it.

Joe was sweaty and tired from the exertion but he felt alive. All his senses were attuned to the woman in front of him. A long tendril of hair clung to her freckle-covered neck. Her breasts rose and fell with each exhalation of breath and her eyes watched him—warily, he thought.

He stunk at the mating dance. He'd always thought he'd gotten lucky that he'd married Mary so young because he didn't like to play the games that men and women played in the getting-to-know-you phase. He preferred honesty and passion.

But they'd already shared too much honesty. Passion now seemed a risky proposition, when lust should never be anything but straightforward—two bodies twisting hotly on the sheets. His body was ready, but his mind warned that this woman would want more than he could comfortably give her.

He understood suddenly why his younger brother, Alex, had dated all those women before meeting and marrying Daisy. If Joe had been doing the same thing since Mary's death, Holly probably wouldn't be affecting him now. Yeah, right.

"What side do I bring out in you, Joe?" she asked.

He regretted his earlier words. But then he'd never been smooth around women.

"A dangerous one."

She walked closer to him. His instincts told him to back away but he didn't. He knew from firsthand experience that once you gave ground it was hard to get it back. Besides, she was a rather slight woman. She didn't scare him.

"Funny, you don't frighten me," she said, tiptoe-ing her fingers up his chest.

She was so close now he could smell her scent. Kind of sweaty, but also sweet. He breathed deeply so that the essence of her was branded on him. Damn. He had to get her into his bed and quick. But he'd never been one to indulge in one-night stands. For him, sex was more than scratching a physical itch.

"I'm not trying to alarm you, I'm just warning you that I don't know myself right now." He'd tried earlier in the car to caution her. Though he knew she was a strong, independent woman, he didn't want to hurt her emotionally. And even the toughest person could be injured by someone whom they cared about. And when he'd touched her leg and she'd stalled her car, he realized she cared more than she wanted to admit.

"That's only fair," she replied, "since you do the same thing to me. Right now I should be concerned with a million things, but the only one I can think of is you."

"Don't say things like that," he said.

"Why not?"

He was trying to be noble. But lust rode him hard and the only thing he could think about was that thin tank top she was wearing and stripping it from her slim body. He wanted—no, needed—to feel her naked flesh under his. He longed to trace the patterned freckles that ran the length of her long neck and disappeared beneath the clinging line of her shirt.

"You might regret them later," he said, because truth was one of the tenets he lived by.

She looked up at him, her blue eyes filled with compassion and understanding. "I doubt that."

"Women always want more than I can give them."

"Even your wife?" she asked.

For a minute he was shocked. No one mentioned Mary to him. It was as if everyone had forgotten her existence. They'd let him create a dark little cave where only he remembered her. He wasn't sure how he felt about having Holly ask him about her.

"I don't talk about my wife." The ball, which he'd been holding, slipped from his hand and rolled to the edge of the driveway. She didn't drop her gaze from his.

"I didn't know that."

"Well, now you do."

The moment had changed and he supposed he should be glad, but he regretted it. Mary was a barrier between them. A very effective one. Why, then, did he feel like a coward for using it?

"I guess we should get you back to your car," Holly said. "I have to be up early in the morning for work."

She walked toward the house and all thoughts about his deceased wife left him. Holly was vibrant and alive in a way that made everything around her pale. Though a part of him was unsure of what he wanted, he knew deep down that there was no indecision. His reluctance was the unwillingness to risk his happiness again. He'd made an odd peace with fate and he didn't want to rock the boat.

"Yes," he said, his voice sounding rusty to him.

She glanced over her shoulder. "Yes, what?"

"Mary wanted more than I could give her."

She didn't move, just watched him with her cat-shaped eyes. "In what way?"

He closed the distance between them and took her slender shoulders in his hands. Her skin was soft and smooth under his. He flexed his fingers, wishing this moment were different. Wishing he could slip his hand under the thin fabric of her T-shirt and feel her skin under his touch. "I'm not exactly sure."

"Then how do you know?"

"There was something in her eyes…. I'm not sure it wasn't disappointment."

"Maybe it was your own feelings projected on her."

He let go. He didn't want to be having this conversation. "What makes you an expert?"

"I didn't say I was."

"Listen, Holly. I've given up on dreams of lifelong love and happiness. But you haven't."

"Maybe right now I'm just looking for a physically satisfying relationship."

"Is that all you look for in a relationship?" he asked, not believing for a second that was the only thing Holly wanted from him.

"Yes," she said, her voice trembling.

"Liar."

She shrugged out of his grasp. "You're right. All around me are women who date casually, but I've never been able to. I don't know if it's because of my family or what...."

Something in her told him that was an excuse she used to protect herself. He wanted to tell her to trust him, but deep inside he wasn't sure he was trustworthy.

"Self-examination is never easy," he said.

"How do you know?"

"Despite the way talk shows and sitcoms make us sound, we guys think about things other than getting laid, sports and beer."

"I know," she said seriously.

"You do?"

"I have brothers."

"Yes, you do. So, where does that leave us?"

"I'm not sure. I feel like if I don't get to know you I'll be missing out on something wonderful."

"Why?"

"Joe, as much as you try to project otherwise, you do have a heart."

He felt as if she'd seen behind his shield to the soft underbelly he'd tried to hide. He'd become an expert at keeping his family at arm's length, trying to protect the part of him that had ached so badly after he'd learned he wasn't a superhero when Mary had died.

"Holly, I don't think I can live up to any mythical expectations."

"I'm not asking you to. I just would like to get to know you."

He was used to analyzing all the angles before making a sound decision, but right now his mind wasn't working. His body ached for hers, and his soul, the part of himself he always tried to ignore, whispered that maybe this woman was worth the risk.

"Will you have dinner with me tomorrow night?" he asked.

She shivered visibly, watching him with her intense gaze. "Okay."

Holly downshifted as she pulled her car up to Baronessa Gelateria. The shop was empty. Empty and dark. She knew from experience the building would be cold too. It seemed whenever a room was vacant it froze from the lack of human warmth.

She'd been lacking that for a long time. She had closeness from her father and brothers but it wasn't the same. What they shared was a deep bond, but she craved something else. Something she'd almost come close to with Joe tonight. Instead, she'd decided to settle for an affair.

"This is it," Joe said, pointing to a BMW sedan. For some reason his choice in cars surprised her. "This is yours?"

"Yes," he said.

"If I'd spent that much money on a car, I'd have gotten a Jag or a Ferrari."

He gave her a half smile that made her blood run heavy and her pulse quicken. Riding in the small car with Joe had been intimate. And they'd shared too much intimacy today.

"I'm not big on flash. This is more practical," he said.

Joe hadn't struck her as a practical guy. She knew that he was CFO of Baronessa, so she figured he had to be pretty serious some of the time. But the Joe she'd met today shouldn't be driving *this* expensive automobile.

"I disagree," she said. Dammit, what was with her tonight?

"You don't know me, Holly."

She glanced away from the car to look at him. "Maybe that's why I can see the real you."

He spread his hands. "I'm the practical one in my family."

That sounded so familiar. Those words had come from her mouth more than once until she'd let a friend talk her into trying something that was just for her. Rock climbing and skydiving. They were daredevil sports that left her feeling alive in a way she hadn't realized another person could make her feel until she'd met Joe.

"You need to define yourself away from your family," she advised him.

"I know who I am," he said firmly.

"I've seen your family in the paper and met Gina today. Your family is bigger than life."

"Not all of us."

"My family is overwhelming too."

"I'm *not* overwhelmed by my family. You make me sound like some kind of wimp."

"I didn't mean it that way."

"Then how did you mean it?"

"It's just... Earlier when your sister was bossing you around, it reminded me of how I treat my brothers sometimes."

"How's that?"

"It doesn't sound nice but I kind of try to shape each of them into a better person than he'd be otherwise."

"You think my family does that to me?"

"I don't know, do they?"

He stared at her in the moonlight and she knew

she'd gone too far. She'd been pushing him all day and now it seemed that nighttime had freed her normally cautious nature.

"Forget I said anything." Who was she to shake the moorings of his world? If he wanted to pretend that his life was peachy-keen, she'd go along with it. She wasn't going to be more significant to him than a few nights of passion.

Still, he just watched her with a quiet intensity. His eyes were so deep and rich that they reminded her of a pot of boiling dark chocolate. The kind she used sparingly to flavor her most exotic pastries at the bakery.

"Be careful, Holly," he said at last.

But caution wasn't in the cards for her tonight. "Why?"

"Because you might get more than you bargained for if you keep pushing me."

"I think I can handle it," she said.

"You think so," he said, leaning closer.

Dammit, he smelled good. A man who'd just won a one-on-one basketball game should smell like a locker room, not like Joe did. Like elemental man. Maybe that was why her self-mastery was lacking.

"I know so," she said, leaning forward herself. He had a nice jaw, square, firm, confident. She wanted to rub her hand across it, but curled her fingers against the urge.

"What makes you so confident?" he asked her.

"Because of your eyes," she said at last.

He didn't say anything, only waited for her to continue. But she couldn't. If she told him what she saw, she'd reveal how much she already liked him. And she wasn't going to do that. The new Holly was a woman who owned her destiny. She didn't wait for fate to shape it.

"Forget it," she said.

He opened the car door, grabbed his clothes and got out. She watched him walk away. He tossed his suit and shoes in the back seat and then turned to her.

"Your eyes tell me something too," he said, unlocking his car and opening the door.

"What?" she asked.

"That I'm not the only one letting other people's expectations shape me."

"You're wrong."

"Prove it. Tell me why I don't frighten you."

She swallowed. She'd felt safe and powerful in her car, but the balance had shifted. Still, she was a woman of her word. She shifted the car into first gear and looked directly at Joe.

Then she told him. "Your appearance is one of suave sophistication but in your eyes I can see your soul. Reflected there is a European sports car barreling down the autobahn."

She stepped on the gas and drove away before he could respond, the night air blowing through her hair. In her mind were all the words she'd wished she'd never said. But caution hadn't been her forte. Tonight that lack may have been her fatal weakness.

Six

Joe's day couldn't have been any slower. For the first time something other than Baronessa Gelati was at the forefront of his mind. He'd spent the day going through the motions but not really being there. Even going so far as begging off lunch with his dad and bagging work on the company's new five-year plan. Instead, he surfed the Internet.

"Got a minute, Joe?" Gina asked from the doorway.

He closed his Internet connection and glanced up at his sister. His brother-in-law Flint was there, as well. "I'm not doing any more press. I don't care what you've convinced Mom of."

Flint laughed and Gina rolled her eyes. "Nothing

like that. I'm taking an informal family poll. Flint wants to do some promo around the annual family reunion.''

''Unless I have to be the family spokesman, I'm all for it. By the way, I think Nick should be the family spokesman. He is the eldest and the COO of Baronessa.''

''Stop using my name in vain, Joe,'' Nick said from the hallway.

Joe lifted his hands innocently. ''Who, me?''

''Great. I'll put the plan in motion,'' Flint said, heading toward the door.

''Coming, Gina?'' Flint asked.

''In a minute.'' Gina watched him with her wide violet gaze, and Joe had the uncomfortable feeling he should have left work early.

''Uh-oh, I'm outta here,'' Nick said, disappearing down the hall.

His sister paced over to the windows and looked down on the street. Joe knew whatever she was going to say he wasn't going to like. He put on his toughest face. The one that made everyone leave him alone.

''What's with that look?'' Gina could always read him.

He shrugged. Sure, he knew he had feelings, but admitting them to the family was something he hated.

''Mom said you disappeared from the gelateria last night with Holly.''

"Why were you talking to Mom about me, Gina?"

"I like my brothers to be happy, Joe. You know that."

"Sure you do. Why the concern?"

"You were acting weird yesterday, even for you."

"Geez, was that a compliment?"

She smiled. Despite her annoying tendencies, he liked his sister. "I just wanted to let you know I'm here. If you need to talk about Holly or anything."

"There's nothing to talk about. Everything's fine."

"Joe, everything hasn't been fine for you since Mary died."

Joe shuddered. That was the first time anyone in his family had said Mary's name to him. Why now? Was he changing, or was the world around him different? Gina watched him with an intensity that made him uncomfortable. Italian women were witchy and superstitious. She'd brought up Mary to see how he'd react.

But he remained expressionless.

"Still stone-faced, I see," she said. "Well, be careful because I know there's a man behind the stone." She walked toward the door.

"Gina, did I try to tell you what to do with Flint?"

"No."

"Then let me do this on my own. I know I'm not Alex but I can handle a woman."

"Okay, big brother," she said, walking out of his office and closing the door behind her.

For once Joe didn't care about his family. Tonight was something between him and Holly—though he knew the evening wouldn't remain a secret.

Especially since he'd chosen Atlantic Fish Co. for dinner. It was one of Boston's most favorite restaurants. It had opened in 1978. He liked the place because of the detailed woodwork and murals of the spirit of the sea. Plus they had intimate, cozy booths.

His mother would find out about the date and then the inquisition would start.

The intercom buzzed.

"Yes, Stella?"

"A Ms. Fitzgerald for you on line one."

Hell, he prayed she wasn't calling to cancel. If he hoped to get anything done at work the rest of the week, he needed to see her tonight and get her out of his mind. His work had been his solace and suddenly thanks to Holly it wasn't.

He picked up line one. "Barone."

"I'm running a little late at the bakery. Where are we going for dinner? Maybe I can meet you there."

Joe wondered if she was really that busy at work or just looking to direct tonight's action. Hell, he didn't blame her. Holly might look fragile but she wasn't. There was a pure fighting spirit in her that would demand she make the most of their time together.

"We're going to Atlantic Fish Co."

"Oh."

"Is something wrong?" he asked.

"I've never been there, but always wanted to try it."

"Why haven't you gone?" he asked.

"It's a couple place not a family place."

"You've never been part of a couple?" he asked.

"Not long enough to get to the stage where you go to a place like that."

Her words sliced through the barrier he'd thought he'd built around his heart, making it beat again. He leaned back in the chair and mentally started making plans.

Tonight was going to be the ultimate in romantic fantasy for Holly Fitzgerald.

Holly changed clothes five times before settling on a slim-fitting dress with little cap sleeves. It was a designer knockoff she'd purchased in an outlet mall. But for tonight she'd splurged on the Enzo sandals she'd had her eye on all season.

She spritzed her body with perfume and checked her appearance one last time before heading for the door. The doorbell rang just as she opened it.

"Ms. Fitzgerald?" the deliveryman asked.

"Yes," she said.

"These are for you." He handed her a lovely bouquet of orchids, calla lilies and a pink flower, which she didn't know the name of. The scents assailed her and she closed her eyes for a minute to enjoy the fresh-cut flowers.

The deliveryman started to leave. "Wait a minute," she said, reaching for her handbag.

"It's all been taken care of," he said and, whistling, walked away.

She closed the door and sank to the deacon's bench along the wall. There was a card. She tugged it free of the pick and turned the paper carefully over in her hands.

She was shaking a little, she realized, and tears burned the back of her eyes. No one had ever sent her flowers. Not her dad when she'd graduated high school. Not her brothers when she'd won the contest. No one had ever thought to send her flowers except Joe Barone. The man who'd told her that he wanted her for only one night.

The note was in his bold, brash handwriting.

Cinderella had until midnight to enjoy her prince, but the magic doesn't have to end for us.

The Joe she'd come to know wasn't the kind of guy who'd feed a woman a line like that, but in her heart she knew she wasn't the kind of woman who could have a red-hot affair.

She had commitments. Commitments to her family and the bakery. Commitments to herself, she realized. But there was nothing that would stop her from enjoying this night with Joe.

The phone rang. She debated answering it, not wanting reality to intrude. But in the end the chance that it could be her dad decided her, and she picked up the phone. "Hello?"

"It's not too late for me to pick you up," Joe said.

"Where are you?"

"About a block from your place."

"I feel like I'm being manipulated. The Atlantic Fish Co. is across town."

"You aren't being manipulated. I'm just being gentlemanly."

"Are you sure?" she asked. Around men she'd never been as confident as she'd like to be.

"Hey, would I lie to you?"

Would he? "I don't know."

Silence buzzed on the line, and she wondered if she'd offended him. It was just that he was a guy who'd learned not to risk his heart, while she might not be looking for happily-ever-after but still believed it existed.

"I guess I'll just have to prove to you that you can trust me."

She shivered at the sincerity in his voice. Oh, God. She was in over her head. "Thanks for the flowers."

"You're welcome."

"I didn't get you anything," she said.

"Your company is gift enough."

"Don't say things like that."

"Why?"

"I might think you mean them. And we decided to go slowly."

"I am going slowly."

"Nothing seems real since the moment we met," she said more to herself than to him.

"I disagree," he said.

She waited.

"Everything finally seems real to me."

Hearing that was sweeter than the flowers he'd sent her. Sweeter than the dinner at Boston's most romantic restaurant. Sweeter than the fire he'd started in her last night. "Oh, Joe."

"Oh, what?"

"I just don't want to disappoint you," she said at last.

"Are you riding with me?" he asked, changing the subject.

She thought maybe Joe didn't really know what to do with her. It made her feel better to think he was as unsure as she was. "Okay."

She disconnected the phone before he could say anything else. She went into the kitchen and got a vase for the flowers, then put them on the counter. The setting summer sun streaming through the window was hot and she closed her eyes for a minute, enjoying its warmth for the first time that day.

The doorbell rang again and this time she hesitated. She'd spent the entire day trying to convince herself he was nothing more than a date, but her heart beat quicker as she walked toward the front of her house. Her pulse raced as she saw his silhouette through the front window.

Everything feminine in her awakened and she realized that these reactions were what she was afraid of. Not Joe or the date, but the way her sentimental heart would react to flowers and a romantic dinner. He'd already told her he wasn't her forever man and she needed to remember that.

She opened the door. Joe was backlit by the setting sun, so the expression on his face was unreadable. But he took a quick breath and reached for her. His fingers trailed down her arm, stopping at her hand. He rubbed his thumb over her knuckles before lifting her hand to his mouth and dropping a warm kiss on the back of it.

''You are beautiful tonight.''

Sensation spread up her arm, making her insides puddle. She was uncomfortable not only with the sensuality he wove around her so effortlessly but also with the sophisticated man standing in front of her. His suit was not a knockoff but a hand-sewn Italian one.

''You are making me feel like Cinderella tonight,'' she said.

''That was my intent.'' He closed her front door and led her down the walk to his car.

She didn't say a word as he seated her and walked around to the driver's side. For this one night she'd forget that in the real world a man like Joe wouldn't really be interested in her. For this one night she'd simply enjoy the fantasy.

"Want to stop by Baronessa's for dessert?" Joe asked as they exited the restaurant.

It was nights like this that made living in Boston worthwhile. The breeze was warm and blew over his skin. Being with Holly sensitized him, making everything seem magnified a hundred times. It was unnerving.

The Atlantic Fish Co. had added to the charm of the evening. Somehow, dining there had created just the romantic atmosphere he'd been hoping for.

She stopped him on the sidewalk, reaching out to grab his hand. Hers was so small in his, he was reminded once again that it was the man's job to protect his woman. But Holly wasn't his...at least not yet.

"I have gelato at my place if you'd rather just go there," she said softly.

Her husky voice brushed over his senses like a match to kindling. The warm breeze around him stirred up his senses. He tugged her closer, so that her body was pressed neatly to his side. Her dress was a fantasy and a nightmare at the same time. Light and frothy, it moved around her as she moved. And he wasn't the only guy who noticed.

Telling himself he had no claim on her didn't work. No matter how much he tried to fool himself into believing that this attraction between them meant nothing, he knew better.

"Let's go," he said.

He seated her in his car and drove quickly through town. Frank Sinatra played quietly in the background. Normally, he favored hard rock but he'd decided tonight called for something else. So he'd broken down and called Alex, figuring even though his brother had settled down with Daisy, the old ladies' man would know what to play on a date.

But in the end it had been their father's advice that Alex had passed on. "The old man swears by Sinatra."

Joe had been reminded again today how much his family really cared for him. Alex had given Joe a list of recommendations for CDs and told him how glad he was that Joe was finally dating again. It was scary to realize that he hadn't been fooling anyone with his stoic mask.

Every damn song on the CD had to do with love— the very last thing he wanted to confront while Holly was in the car with him. From now on he was listening to hard rock.

"Is this Sinatra?" she asked.

"Yes, one of his early recordings."

"I've never listened to his stuff much."

Joe took his gaze from the road for just a minute. "You can't grow up Italian and not listen to Old Blue Eyes."

"I can imagine. So what was it like being one of eight children?"

"Craziness most of the time."

"For me too. But the boys were younger so I could distance myself a little from them."

"Did it work?" Growing up, he'd felt protected being surrounded by his siblings and parents. Everything in his life had seemed charmed until Mary's sickness.

"Probably not as well as I've always thought it did."

"What do you mean?" he asked. Holly was an enigma. Frail and ethereal on the outside, tough as nails on the inside. Except there was a part of her that was very soft. That part was clear in her eyes tonight.

"Just that even when I was the older sister pretending to be bothered by the boys, I still spent the majority of my time at home with them. I've always liked taking care of my brothers."

"Do you take care of your family?" he asked. She'd carefully kept the conversation away from her dad tonight and he knew it had been deliberate. But because there had been subjects he too hadn't wanted to discuss, he'd let her.

"Most of the time."

"Who takes care of you?" he asked. She looked like someone who needed pampering and had never been indulged.

She was silent for a minute, her serious face illuminated in the flashing lights of the street lamp. "I do."

"Have you ever thought about letting someone else do it?"

"Have you?"

He braked to a stop for a traffic light and glanced over at her. He didn't like how easily she saw into his soul. "I'm a man."

"Oh, so it's different for you," she said. Her words sounded solemn, but he sensed the laughter beneath them.

"Of course it's different. Men are expected to suck it up and shoulder on."

"Women are too."

"But no one thinks less of you if you lean on a man."

"I think if two people really love each other then leaning on each other is the best thing in the world."

"I thought you didn't believe in love."

"Of course I believe it exists...for some people."

"Not you?"

"I don't know. I can't fall in love now."

"Why not?"

"Dad's health insurance is still iffy and I've got obligations to fulfill. Love takes time and effort. Two things I don't have."

Joe concentrated on driving, pulling into her neighborhood and finally her driveway. "Maybe you haven't met the right man."

"There's no maybe about it."

"Really?" he asked. "Then what about me?"

Seven

Holly took a deep breath, fumbling in her purse for her keys. She wasn't about to think of Joe Barone and Mr. Right in the same breath. Illusion, she reminded herself. That was all he had to offer her. Her fancy dress and the nice dinner they'd just shared made her feel like Cinderella. Midnight was only a few strokes away and then the magic would end.

Her first instinct was to hedge and duck, but she'd never really been able to follow through on it. She liked dealing honestly with those around her. ''You think you could be my Mr. Right?''

''I don't want to be ruled out of the running,'' he said. His voice was deep and husky, brushing over her senses and making her remember how long it had been since she'd shared whispers with a man.

And she brought a lot of baggage with her. One-night stands and red-hot affairs were one thing; Mr. Right was forever, and forever was scary. "I'm not sure you'd really want to be."

"Why not?"

"Because there's a part of you that you keep locked inside."

"The surly part?" he asked almost teasingly.

"I wish I could joke about this but you asked me about my dreams."

His face was stark in the shadowed light provided by the street lamp. She felt as if she'd crossed a line that neither of them even wanted to admit existed but she knew it did. Life had taught her that nothing lasted, that nothing was ever really secure and that the unexpected was closer than it seemed.

"Your dreams aren't a joke," he said.

"I know. They're all I have."

He put his hand on her thigh, and a flash of sexual desire flooded her body. She was ultrasensitized to his touch, and each caress—even the most innocent one—sent shock waves through her system. "I want to make your dreams come true."

She knew he could. His eyes promised dark dreams of carnal delight—but she wanted more.

"Let's talk about this inside," she said.

She got out of the car before he could open her door. His footsteps were heavy as he followed her up the walk to her small house. She unlocked the door and led him inside.

The kitchen was the biggest room in the house, and her favorite. She had a professional-grade oven and a large island in the middle. "Have a seat and I'll get the gelato."

"Thanks."

He slid out of his jacket and loosened his tie.

"I made some butter cookies last night. I'll get those out too," she said. From the first they'd been able to banter, but now they were reduced to inane small talk that made her wish she'd never brought up the subject of Mr. Right.

"Why don't you go wait in the living room," she said. She needed a few minutes to compose herself.

His sharp gaze told her he wasn't fooled. "Sure."

She prepared dishes of gelato and a plate of cookies as well as snifters of cognac. She picked up the tray and entered the living room, setting it on the coffee table. Joe wasn't seated as she'd hoped but studying the pictures on the wall.

Holly wasn't sure she liked him seeing her family. This man whom she wanted to have a passionate affair with shouldn't know the personal details of her life. Not if he only intended for them to be together for the short term.

"Here's dessert," she said.

"Your family looks close," he said, walking toward her.

"We are."

She cleared her throat, not sure what to say next. She smiled at him. Maybe he'd forgotten about the whole Mr. Right thing. She certainly wished she could. She realized that this man was really her ideal man. The one she'd secretly dreamed about since her mother had died and she'd been left with the boys to raise. The one she'd been hoping to meet since she'd started dating and realized that real men weren't the same as dream men. The one she'd come to know as a man of honor.

Joe handed her a snifter and took a seat next to her. She could feel his warmth, he sat so close to her. She shivered a little and resisted the urge to slide closer to him on the couch. It would be so easy to do. The leather was slippery against her silk dress, and if she shifted her weight, she'd coast right up against him.

He'd unfastened the top button of his shirt. Tufts of hair were visible through the opened collar. She reached out toward him before realizing what she was doing, then dropped her hand and looked up.

Joe stared at her with that mesmerizing dark gaze that made her feel exposed…vulnerable.

"What?" she asked.

"Why did you stop?" he asked.

"I'm not sure where we stand."

"I am. You told me about your dreams. Now let me tell you mine."

"Yours?"

He nodded. The lambent desire in his eyes made her pulse run heavier. "I envision the two of us—"

She put her fingers over his lips. She didn't want

to hear what he had to say. She wanted him, but she wanted—no, needed—to pretend that he was her dream man for this one night. She knew he wasn't. She knew this could never last. But for this one night she wanted to believe it.

She searched to find her voice. ''I don't want to be too forward.''

''Honey, I don't think you could be.''

She wasn't sure she wanted to be given free license to his body. But she did want to touch him. She reached for him again, this time brushing her fingertips along the edge of his jaw and down his throat. His Adam's apple bobbed as she moved her hand over it.

His gaze held hers and she felt she was drowning in Joe. His heat, his soul, his body all called to her, making her forget everything about herself except that she had this one night as a magical princess. This one night that her fairy godmother had given her and she didn't want to waste it.

He took her snifter from her and placed it on the table. Taking her face in his hands, he caressed it, touching her cheeks, tracing the line of her nose and then finally rubbing gently against her lower lip. Her mouth tingled. She licked her lips and tasted the edge of his thumb.

Bending, he tilted her head back and brushed his lips against hers. They'd kissed before, so this should be no big deal, but Holly felt as if this time something deeper was happening.

Magic, she realized.

His mouth moved on hers with a quiet strength. There was passion, of course, but also something more like affection. And that caring made the difference to her. A well opened deep inside. She framed his face with her hands and took control of the kiss.

Joe pulled away slowly, his lips and tongue leaving her mouth.

"Are you sure about this, Holly?"

It had been a long time since Joe had felt this rush of physical desire. The gentlemanly behavior he'd carefully cultivated over the years was stripped away, leaving in its place a primal man.

This was just one more awakening that she'd brought about in him. He'd been frozen, locked away from life for so long.

He watched her, staring at him. Her eyes were luminous and wide, dominating her entire face. Her freckled skin was flushed. He trailed an unsteady hand down her bare arm, tracing one of the many patterns on her skin.

As his blood pounded an ancient rhythm in his head, his noble ideas of slow, romantic seduction slipped away. He didn't miss them, and watching Holly through narrowed eyes, he didn't think she would either.

Her breath rushed in and out, forcing her breasts to strain against the silk bodice of her dress. Her hardened nipples were prominent through the thin fabric. She still hadn't spoken but he couldn't resist touching her.

He rubbed his thumb over one distended nipple. When she moved more fully into his touch, he cupped her breast. Between his thumb and forefinger he lightly rubbed her nipple. Holly moaned deep in her throat.

The sound made his flimsy control disappear. It had been so long since he'd had the solace of a woman's body, so long since he'd given in to the physical side of his nature that he didn't know if he could restrain himself. Didn't know if he could bring her along with him.

"It's been a long time for me," he said at last.

Her crystalline-blue gaze met his. "Me too."

"I mean it, honey. I locked this part of myself away."

She sat up. "Are you telling me you haven't had sex since your wife died?"

He rubbed his forehead and looked away. "Yes."

She didn't say anything and he was afraid he may have finally found the way to slow the pace. Damn, he didn't want to leave now. But she cupped his face in her hands and brought his mouth to hers. The kiss she gave him was full of passion and caring. More caring than a man who felt as shaky as Joe did deserved.

"I promise it won't be painful," she said.

He laughed. "It could be quick."

"That's okay with me."

"I want to take my time with you."

"There's always next time," she whispered.

Next time. The words were the balm he needed to indulge himself in Holly's sweet body. To take what they both needed. This wasn't a romantic fairy tale that demanded perfection. They were both human and understood that need sometimes was just that. Need. And control wasn't something that could be counted on.

Her hands on his head urged him closer to her bosom. He lowered his mouth to her turgid nipple and blew lightly on it. It tightened even further and Joe could wait no longer to take her in his mouth. The barrier of her dress served to heighten the sensation and at the same time to frustrate him. He sucked harder, pulling her deep into his mouth. He used his hand to cup her other breast, rubbing his forefinger over her nipple.

Her hands left his head and massaged his back. "Joe, I want to feel you."

"How do you get out of this damn dress?" He too wanted flesh upon flesh. He needed it. He needed to feel this moment in blinding Technicolor and not the dull gray his world had become.

Holly shimmied out of her dress, leaving her clad in only those damned gorgeous freckles of hers and a pair of panties so scanty that he couldn't think of anything but getting back to her body, removing that last barrier and joining them so deeply, so tightly that neither of them would ever be free.

He sat up, pulled off his tie and unbuttoned his shirt in quick, hurried movements, then tossed it away. He kicked off his shoes and removed the condom he'd put in his wallet earlier. Holly just lay there watching him.

He unfastened his pants and pushed them and his briefs off his legs. Standing naked in front of her, he felt everything in him swell. His groin was so hard, his muscles were flooded with strength and he felt like a warrior who'd been away too long and finally had come home.

Only home wasn't a place. It was one fragile woman who watched him with radiant eyes and opened arms and legs. He knelt next to her and caressed her skin. Her flesh tightened under his touch, shivers of sensation visible in the way she quaked.

He felt powerful and masculine. The need to savor her battled with the need to bury himself in her humid warmth. He spread his fingers and ran his hand down the length of her midriff and stomach. Her muscles tightened as he slid past her tiny waist and neared the waistband of her panties.

He slipped one finger under the elastic, searching for the center of her desire. He found it and teased it with a soft touch.

She moaned again. "I thought you were in a hurry."

He had been. Until he realized that exploring Holly was more important than giving in to the maddening need to climax inside her. Right now he needed to know all her secrets.

"I changed my mind."

He pushed her panties down her legs and she kicked them aside. She grabbed the condom from his fingers, tore it open and sheathed his aching flesh. ''I can't wait, Joe.''

He nodded. She tugged him up and over her. Propping himself on one elbow, he used his other hand to test her readiness. Though he knew she was eager, he wanted to make sure her body was ready for him. She was warm and wet when he slid his finger into her. She lifted her hips, beckoning him closer. He adjusted himself, braced himself on his forearms and slid inside her.

He stopped when he was hilt deep inside her and looked down at her. She watched him, eyes wide open. Her hands clasped his buttocks and urged him to move, but he waited, teasing the both of them for a long minute.

When her hips shifted beneath him, he started to thrust. Watching her carefully, he brought her along with him. Everything in his body tightened, and he felt his climax building at the base of his spine. He reached between their bodies and touched her once and then twice. She dug her nails into his back and then let out a moan of completion, her body tightening around his.

He shifted, held her hips and thrust quickly into her three times before he climaxed as well. His body was drained of everything. Slowly reality came back to him and he realized he'd just lowered a barrier he'd never meant to lower.

Holly hadn't felt this free since the first time she'd skydived. She held Joe tightly to her, aware that she never wanted to let go. She pressed her face into his shoulder so he couldn't see how deeply she'd been affected by his lovemaking.

She'd experienced good sex before but this went beyond good. She felt completely exposed to Joe, and that caused a chill of apprehension in the pit of her stomach. She'd been too used to taking care of herself and now she'd let someone inside the wall of caring that she generally reserved for her family.

But maybe luck was on her side and Joe would snuggle with her. This was her magical night, after all, she reminded herself. Her night of illusion with a genuine Prince Charming.

But instinct told her that the illusion was over and that reality was waiting in the wings.

Joe shifted on her, pulling his body from hers. A cold chill shook her even before he levered himself up off her. She crossed her arms over her chest and pressed her legs together. Joe watched her through half-lidded eyes, as if each move she made was being recorded in his mind.

"Where are you going?" she asked.

"To get rid of the condom," he said without meeting her gaze.

He padded silently out of the room. He was a solid, muscular man and she was amazed that she hadn't taken more time to explore him. She'd been overwhelmed by the lust in each of his touches. He'd carried her along in a wake of desire and passion until she'd forgotten everything.

But it seemed the time to remember was upon

them. She sat up and tugged the chenille throw off the back of the couch, wrapping it around her body. What should she do? For the first time she was uncomfortable in her own home.

He reentered the room and started to dress. She couldn't believe it. He was going to abandon her. She glanced at the melting gelato in the ice-cream cups and knew she wasn't going to just let him leave.

"Joe?"

He fastened his trousers and looked at her. She hesitated, unsure what to say. How did you ask a man to stay with you when it was obvious he wanted to leave?

"I'm sorry, but I've got to get out of here," he said.

His face was shuttered, showing her no emotions at all, and she felt the way she had the day they met, when she'd heard him say he didn't want to spend the day with her.

She wished she had something other than her dress to put on, feeling distinctly defenseless wrapped in the blanket. She didn't want to leave the living room because she knew he'd leave without saying goodbye. And she needed to talk to him.

"Why?" she asked.

"I just do. Listen, I'll call you," he said, picking up his shirt and shrugging into it.

"Will you sit down with me for a minute?" she asked.

He froze. In his eyes she saw that he didn't want to do anything but get away. Find someplace private and restore himself.

She held her hand out to him and slowly he took it. She drew him down to her side. He sat as stiffly as she had earlier this evening. The irony of the moment wasn't lost on her.

"Don't think about it," she said, trying to figure out what he needed from her.

He reached out toward her cheek but dropped his hand before he touched her. "I wish it were that easy."

"You said yourself we should just enjoy this thing between us and take it one moment at a time."

"That doesn't mean I was right." He stood and walked to the front door.

His leaving hurt worse than anything she'd experienced at the hands of the opposite sex. Even being stood up the night of her senior prom paled in comparison.

"What bothers you the most, Joe?" she asked. "That you had sex with me or that you enjoyed it?"

He pivoted to face her. Maybe she'd gone too far but she wasn't sure how to get through the protective layer he'd donned the minute he'd pulled out of her body. She wasn't used to letting men use her.

When he said nothing, she said, "I don't think Mary expected you to quit living."

"I haven't."

"Yes, you have. Everyone is too afraid of your scowl to tell you, but they all know it."

He stalked back to her side. He was angry but she sensed not with her.

"What do you want from me?" he asked, his voice crude.

"Perception is too much to ask, huh?" She didn't want to say that it had been a long time for her too. That no man had ever blown into her life the way Joe had and then shaken her the way his presence had. She didn't want to watch him walk away because she had the feeling she'd never see him again.

"I'm trying not to hurt you," he said.

"That's funny because leaving is what hurts me the most."

"I never wanted that."

There was something so sad in his eyes that her heart melted. She reached out for him, took his hand in hers and tugged him down the hall to her bedroom. He paused for a minute, resisting her, then sighed and gave in. Only the moon lit the room, and the shadows were comforting because she didn't have to face the fact that she'd done the one thing she'd sworn she'd never do again. She'd cheapened herself for a man who didn't want her as much as she wanted him.

Eight

Joe never thought of himself as a weak man until this moment. He knew that he shouldn't follow her. But he felt a bit as if he imagined Adam had when Eve had offered him the apple. Mind saying one thing, body saying something else entirely.

Staying would only make things worse. And as much as he longed to comfort himself in Holly's arms, he wasn't sure he could afford to pay for the pleasure.

For his own good and Holly's he should leave. But the temptation of her sweet curves was too great to resist. He admitted to himself he didn't really even try.

Once in her bedroom, she dropped the blanket

she'd used to cover her body. Gradually her long limbs and slender curves were revealed in the moonlight. Her freckled skin was barely visible but he knew the patterns from earlier on her couch when he'd made her his. The image of her creamy skin was branded in his brain, and he'd never be able to envision her again without being reminded of it.

She stood before him more vulnerable than any woman should ever be. If he'd learned one thing from his father it was that men protected the women. And he'd done a poor job of protecting Holly. Though he strongly believed everyone controlled their own happiness, he'd dealt her a strong blow and she'd snapped back, reacting with caring.

Oh, God, could it be more than caring?

Joe removed his clothing quickly. Whatever was going on in Holly's head, he needed to let her know she wasn't alone. That he too was unable to resist the web of passion that ensnared them. She seemed so fragile standing in front of him with no defenses, but he realized she'd been the stronger of the two.

She'd been the one to reach past her hurt and take him by the hand. Leading him from the brink of self-reproach and regret. Leading him to her bedroom. Leading him, it seemed to his greatest weakness. But if he was staying, he was going to enjoy every minute of it and not think. Not remember. Not call himself a bastard.

The room was hidden in shadows and though normally he preferred to make love with the lights on, he welcomed the darkness. Welcomed the chance to take Holly again without looking into those crystal-blue eyes of hers.

"I did promise the magic wouldn't end at midnight," he said, taking her hands in his.

"Is that what you call sex—magic?" she asked. Something quivered in her voice, and Joe thought maybe she was regretting leading him down the hall.

It was too late now. Too late to keep from inflicting the pain. But he could soften the blow. "With you, I do."

"Oh, Joe."

He pulled her closer in his arms, wrapping himself around her. He needed her. Needed her in a way that went beyond physical. And that scared him, because he was a logical man.

"Let me make love to you," he said.

She nodded. He lifted her in his arms and carried her to the bed. He held her with one arm and flipped the covers back with another. Setting her in the middle of the bed, he realized darkness wasn't going to work for them. He needed to see her. To memorize every reaction she had.

"Where's the light switch?" he asked.

"No lights. Come to bed, Joe," she said, grasping his wrist and holding him in place.

He could have easily escaped her hold. He worked out twice a day and could bench-press more than she weighed. More than her touch held him in place. "I want to see you."

She tightened her grip on him and spoke so softly he had to strain to hear her words.

"You've already seen too much."

Her words struck through his tough-guy exterior and he sank to the bed. He pulled her into his arms and savored the feel of her pressed full-length against him. He lowered his head and took her lips, thrusting his tongue leisurely into her mouth. Her tongue teased him with shy touches, driving him to the brink.

He slid down her body, leaving his mouth on her skin, savoring Holly. Her skin was smooth, scented and hot under his lips.

This was ridiculous. He was a grown man, not a teenager, but he was aching to bury himself deep inside her again, as if it had been days since they'd last made love instead of only minutes. What was she doing to him?

Her hands swept down his chest, stopping when she met the blunt tip of his arousal. "I see you recover quickly."

He caressed his way to her center. Humid warmth greeted him. The rest of her tasted so good that he was powerless to resist knowing all of her. Besides, he wanted this night to be enchantment for her. "This is fast even for me."

"Must be that magic you were talking about earlier."

"Or it might be something else entirely," he said.

"What?" she asked.

Her fingers tightened around his shaft in a way that was making him forget this evening wasn't all about his pleasure. What the hell had she said?

He kissed her deeply and then skimmed his tongue down her body, lingering to suckle at each of her breasts. Her nipples were hard and her breasts ripe. He cupped her, squeezing gently while he drew deeply on her flesh. Deep in his soul he felt he was getting some form of sustenance from her. Something life-sustaining.

She was moaning, her hands running up and down his back, lingering at his buttocks. He groaned, unsure how much longer he could last. He grabbed her hands, manacled her wrists in his grip above her head. Then he moved farther down her body.

He kissed her abdomen, brushed his lips against the springy curls that hid her secrets from him. Secrets he'd come close to unraveling earlier. But this time he wanted more than a fleeting glimpse at them. He wanted to explore and discover the very heart of Holly.

He freed her hands, sweeping his touch up and down her body. She raised her hips, bringing her warm center more fully into contact with his mouth. He sought the point of all her pleasure and teased it with the tip of his tongue. When her hands gripped his head tightly, he scraped his teeth along the nerve center and felt her go over for him.

She called his name. Her thighs squeezed his shoulders and her body convulsed in his hands. She was magnificent. She was beautiful. She was tugging at him. And he slid up over her and thrust into her warm body while the tremors of her climax still rocked her.

Her hands came up to hold his head, and she brought her lips to his and kissed him deeply. The magic he'd promised her seemed to fill the room. He felt it flow from her mouth to his as everything in his soul reached forward toward her. They moved in unison until they climaxed, this time together.

Joe didn't have words to speak or energy to think but he knew something mystical had happened in this bedroom and it frightened him more than anything he'd ever faced before.

The alarm went off at five o'clock the next morning. Holly jerked from sleep as she always did and reached for the off button, stopping when she encountered warm, male flesh.

Joe.

Oh, God.

She levered herself up on an elbow and reached across his body to shut off the radio. He groused in his sleep but didn't waken, which she was thankful for. She sat up and the sheets slid down his body.

She resisted the urge to rub her fingers along his biceps. Even resting, it was strong, solid. Much like the man himself. He was so big that it never occurred to her that he might have a weakness. Until last night.

He hadn't made love to a woman since his wife's

death. Until her. She felt overwhelmed by that. Overwhelmed by the fact that she'd moved something in him that other women hadn't. Overwhelmed by the fact that it might mean more to her than she should let it.

There was something about a well-built man that got to her. Only this time he'd found his way past her defenses before she'd seen his six-pack and deltoids. Dammit. She was almost thirty. When was she going to stop making decisions with her heart instead of her head? Like she had with Roger, her guitar playing ex-boyfriend who'd let her support him for three years.

Except her head didn't understand how lonely it was taking care of everyone all the time. She got out of bed before she did something really stupid like call in sick to work and stay home with Joe. Joe needed her. The way he'd turned to her the second time they'd made love had stirred a part of her soul that she'd never let anyone see.

The sex had been incredible, but sleeping with him was what had made her throat close up with suppressed emotion. Her other lovers hadn't cuddled her close. They hadn't wrapped their bodies around hers and cupped her breasts in their hands while they'd slept. Joe had. His face had nestled into her neck so that she felt each breath he took. She'd been surrounded by him, and as she stood next to the bed now, she realized how cold she felt without him.

Get used to it, she ordered herself.

Quietly, she got clean underwear from her dresser and padded into the bathroom. Maybe she could sneak out of the house before he awoke. She'd leave him a note.

Except she wasn't a coward. Never had been and didn't intend to start now. She'd made her decision to fight for Joe last night when he'd turned to walk away from her.

Entering the bathroom, she turned the water on and waited for it to get warm. She was concentrating intently on her day, trying to pretend it was almost normal to wake up with a man in her bed. Only it wasn't just any man in her bed.

It was Joe Barone. Joe, who wasn't even close to someone she'd ordinarily meet, much less date. He came from another world. Hell, she'd known that when she'd accepted his invitation. Now she understood why Cinderella had left at midnight. She hoped it had been easier for Cinderella to deal with reality in the early hours of morning, because it sure as heck wasn't easy for Holly.

The door opened and Joe stuck his tousled head around the doorjamb. "Is this a private shower?"

She shook her head. He looked like a cover model standing in the doorway. He propped his arm against the door frame and stood there unconcerned about his nudity. She hadn't taken her time last night to look her fill, but she did this morning.

His chest was covered in a smattering of dark hair that tapered down to his...very eager manhood. She smiled despite herself. One thing was distinct—whatever might be keeping them apart emotionally didn't affect them physically.

She glanced up and met his gaze. He winked at her. "Yeah, you do that to me."

It seemed that the passion of the night before hadn't been exorcised as she'd hoped. Instead, her entire body seemed to jump to alert. Her skin felt sensitized, her breasts full and heavy, and between her legs there was a dampness.

"Holly?"

She realized she'd been staring at him. "Sorry. I don't know the rules for this kind of thing."

"There aren't any. Just do what feels right."

"Is that what you're doing?" she asked.

"I'm certainly not thinking."

Did he regret last night? She'd made him stay. Oh, why had she done that? She turned away and tested the water, which was steaming up the bathroom.

She stepped into the shower quickly, lathered herself and started to rinse before Joe joined her. She handed him the soap. She'd never showered with another person before. She knew the shower had the potential to be very sensual, but she couldn't do that right now. Her body ached from last night and inside she felt quivery. There was a part of herself she'd always managed to keep protected from the men she'd dated. A part that only Joe had touched.

He watched her as warily as she watched him, it

seemed. Two battered souls, she thought. Both longing for comfort but still afraid to reach out.

"Can I rinse?" he asked. The question was mundane, the actions that accompanied it were anything but. His body rubbed against hers as they maneuvered in the small shower. Her nipples throbbed and she wanted to press herself against him.

But she couldn't. There was work and she didn't want to have sex with him again until she'd had time to think. Time to figure out if the sex had been as sacred as it had felt in the middle of the night.

She pushed the curtain back and got out of the shower without washing her hair. She toweled dry and pulled her underwear on in record speed, then braided her hair. She heard the water stop.

"I'll get you a towel," she said and escaped down the hall.

Holly tossed a towel through the door and didn't reenter the steamy bathroom. He was hard and aching and wanted nothing more than to bury himself in her sweet heat one more time. But it was clear she was putting up fences that said No Trespassing.

He stared at himself in the mirror, hardly recognizing the man he saw there. Hell, he didn't blame her. He had wanted to get away and lick his wounds in private, but she'd stopped him. Last night hadn't been his smartest move, yet he didn't regret it. He'd never wanted any woman as much as he'd wanted Holly. Maybe not even Mary.

"Joe, I've got to go," she said through the door. She sounded tired and unsure. Not at all like the Holly Fitzgerald he'd come to know. For the first time he looked objectively at their relationship. He'd been kidding himself that one night of sex with her would be enough. That one night would make the ache for her go away. That one night would enable him to get back to normal.

Normal had disappeared the first time she'd walked in the door, and he wasn't sure he missed it. He only knew that he had to figure out how to make these new feelings not so unsteady. He needed a plan. He'd approach it the same way he did an amortization. Rules and limits had to be established.

He wrapped the towel around his waist and opened the door. Just once he'd like to have a relationship with a woman in which everything went smoothly. Or at least appeared to. Even his life with Mary hadn't been smooth before her illness.

She stood in front of him in her chef's uniform—dark pants and white shirt. There was nothing sexy about a plain white unisex shirt. His mind knew that but his body said that when it was Holly's body underneath, of course there was.

"Can you give me five minutes to dress? I'll leave with you." Her hair was caught back in a braid and her long neck was visible at the top of her shirt. He saw the slight discoloration on her neck and remembered giving her that love bite in the middle of the night when they were both more asleep than awake.

"I didn't mean to disturb you," she said softly.

"Too late," he said. She'd woken the sleeping beast and Joe wasn't sure how he felt about that. Last night had shattered a part of himself that he'd always felt confident of. But in her arms he'd had no control, no boundaries, and that made him question the truths of whom he was.

"I'm sorry. Do you need a lot of sleep?" she asked. If she were in his bed, he wouldn't waste a minute sleeping—ever. He'd make each night as incredible as last night had been.

"No." He never had. Even as a child he'd been a night owl and up with the sun. Four hours were the most he'd ever needed. It had come in handy when Mary had been so sick. He'd rarely left her side.

"Then what'd you mean?" she asked.

He wasn't sure he wanted her to know how deeply she'd affected him. But those damn crystal eyes of hers looked sad and he knew she needed to hear the truth. "You disturbed my soul."

She blanched and took a step back. "I have no idea where we're going to end up. We were talking about one night."

"I know. That's why we're both dancing around each other like two prizefighters. Each knows the other's strengths and weaknesses."

"Now what?" she asked.

He didn't answer her. He'd forgotten what it was like to have to protect someone weaker than he was. What if he let her down the way he had Mary? He didn't know if he could give his soul to a woman again. To plan to be her mate and then watch her slip slowly from his grasp.

He dressed quickly, noticing that Holly kept her gaze firmly away from him but didn't leave the room. He realized then that neither of them knew what to do here or how to react. He needed a plan, but at the moment he just needed some distance.

He sat to put on his shoes and Holly looked at him again. She wrapped her arms around her waist and watched him with wide eyes that made him want to protect her from the world. He stood and opened his arms.

Holly hesitated.

"Come on, baby. I won't hurt you."

Her eyes said it was too late and the damage had already been done. But she took a step toward him. It gave him hope.

"We'll figure this out. We just need a plan."

She stopped. "A plan. What is this, a business merger?"

He hadn't considered that. A business merger. What a great idea. He added it to the variables he already had in the back of his head. The file labeled Holly and Joe.

"No, but if we treat it like one I think we'll both come out of it whole."

She shook her head sadly. Her arms dropped from her waist and her hands curled into fists. "You don't believe that, do you?"

He realized she was angry. He didn't blame her. But he was helpless to react as anything other than the man the past had taught him to be. "I have to, Holly. It's the way I've learned to live."

She closed the gap between them and stood toe-to-toe with him. She tapped his chest with her index finger. "That's not living, that's hiding."

"Are you calling me a coward?" he asked, his own anger building.

"No... Well, yes, I guess I am."

"I'd punch a man if he called me that."

"Do whatever makes you feel better. But the truth is something you can't fight your way out of."

"I'm not delusional."

"I never said you were. Just that it's easier for you to hide than to face life."

"I lead a very full life."

"I'm not saying you don't. Just that you don't *live* it."

"What do you want from me?"

She narrowed her eyes and skimmed them over his frame. "Just for you to be the man you were last night."

"What man was that?"

"One who didn't analyze with his mind what he knew in his heart."

"I don't have a heart anymore, Holly."

"Then I guess this is goodbye."

"No. Not goodbye. Not yet."

He tugged her into his arms. He held her close,

ignoring the arousal she drew from him so easily, and concentrated instead on the fresh clean scent of her. He wanted to absorb her into his skin.

"I'll call you tonight and we'll work this out," he said.

"Will we?"

"Trust me."

She didn't say anything else, just walked out of her house. He followed her car to work, watching her drive with abandon. Twice she was almost in an accident. He was sweating by the time she'd pulled into Kirkpatrick's Bakery. And he knew then that he couldn't fall for Holly. If he did, he'd never have another moment's peace.

Nine

Two days later Joe still hadn't called.

Why would he? Holly asked herself. She'd called him a coward and driven him away. No man wanted to face his own weakness, much less be with a woman who pointed it out. Hadn't she learned anything from her brothers?

Joe wasn't the only one who was hiding. She'd worked late at the bakery the first day, and then spent the night at her dad's house because the boys couldn't be there. Deep inside she knew she'd been hiding from Joe the first day.

Still, he hadn't tried to get in touch.

He had to be running scared. She'd felt the same way after she'd left him. The entire morning at the bakery she'd taken her frustration out on the rolls and bread. Instead of using the new kneading machine, she'd kneaded by hand, hoping to clear her mind by putting her hands to work.

But her mind still wasn't clear. Joe was an enigma and she wasn't going to be satisfied until she understood what made him tick. He made her feel like more than some fairy-tale princess. He made her believe that dreams were still viable and sometimes really did come true. She wasn't going to give him up that easily.

Holly had called his office twice. Once, early in the morning, he'd been in a meeting. The second time he'd been in the office but unable to take her call. Since she didn't know where he lived, she made the decision to go and wait in the lobby for Joe.

She got there just after five and watched the building empty of workers. Joe's car was still parked in his reserved spot. She left her car and walked to the doors.

She wasn't sure she'd made the right choice in coming. She told herself to stay home. To respect his silence and let go. But Joe had touched a place deep inside her where she'd never been touched before, and letting go wasn't an option.

Baronessa's executive headquarters were near the Prudential Center on Huntington Avenue. She had no reason to be in this part of town. She couldn't pretend she was in the neighborhood and decided to drop by. Besides, she didn't want to be dishonest.

Entering the building, she wasn't sure what to do. Hang out in the lobby until he left? What if one of the security guards asked her what she was doing here?

That would be too embarrassing and way too weird for her. She turned to leave but stopped when she saw all the pictures on the wall. There were plaques, as well, for all the awards Baronessa had won over the years for their gelato.

It seemed odd that after so many years in the business they'd have problems with one of their flavors as they had earlier this year. But a part of her was very grateful they had, otherwise she wouldn't have won their new-flavor contest and met Joe.

Small brass plates under each picture detailed the people in them. Joe's history was here. On this wall he passed every day was his life. She studied it, looking for clues as to why he was running from her.

"Holly?"

She turned. Joe looked every inch the business executive in his Hugo Boss suit and sedate tie. Signs of fatigue were visible around his eyes. He watched her wearily and she wondered again if she'd made the right decision.

"Hi, Joe."

"What are you doing here?" he asked. He took a step closer to her as the elevator opened and a group of people moved by them.

Taking a deep breath, she said, "I got tired of waiting for your call."

The elevator emptied again and more people streamed past them. Holly felt their curious gazes on her as they walked by. Okay, this really was a bad idea.

"I'm sorry. I shouldn't have come."

She started toward the lobby doors, but Joe's hand on her shoulder stopped her. She could feel the heat from his touch right through her thin rayon sundress. It radiated downward from her shoulder, spreading gooseflesh along her arm and tightening her nipples.

This was why she'd come. She missed his touch. She missed his eyes, so dark and guarded but burning with desire.

"Let's go someplace private where we can talk," Joe said.

"Do you have time?" Holly asked.

He cupped her elbow and led her toward the elevators. "Yes."

"I tried to call earlier."

"It's been a crazy couple of days," he said.

They entered the elevator and Joe hit the button for five.

"Is that why you didn't call?"

He glanced at her. His hand was now on her elbow, his fingers rubbing slowly back and forth, making thinking nearly impossible.

"No."

"Maybe I shouldn't have come today," she said, tugging free of his grasp.

"I'm glad you did."

"Why?"

"Because I just realized how much I've missed you."

"Really?"

He nodded.

"Then why didn't you call me?" she asked angrily.

He hit the emergency-stop button. "I know you're upset with me and you have every right to be. But dammit, woman—"

"Don't swear at me."

He pulled her into his arms and bent his head, whispering words she couldn't understand. But her soul understood the message in his embrace. He held her so closely and so tightly that she thought he didn't ever want to let go. She held him just as securely, realizing that maybe he wanted her as much as she wanted him. Maybe he needed her in his life as much as she needed him. Despite the comfort of his arms, that scared the hell out of her.

Joe held Holly tighter to him, realizing as he did so that the frozen barrier he'd used to protect his heart was melting. After being cold and alone for so long, he'd finally found the woman who could waken him. His Persephone bringing spring.

His feelings roared through him, laying waste to the excuses he'd used to keep his distance from her. The reasons he'd been using to justify taking this woman and making her his and then not calling. Laying waste to the lies he'd used to protect himself. In one minute he realized that he hadn't protected himself at all.

He bent and took her mouth in a kiss that said all the things he was afraid to say out loud. She responded reluctantly, it seemed to him. He leaned against the wall of the elevator and held her tighter, then lifted her off her feet and thrust his tongue deep in her mouth.

She moaned, tilted her head to the side and cupped his face with her hands. Those small, slender hands that had wrought magic on his frozen soul.

Arousal rushed through him—strong, powerful and unwilling to be denied. He shifted his legs, lifted her higher into the cradle of his thighs. Her legs parted and he was nestled against the center of her. Damn, she went to his head faster than ninety-proof whiskey. He set her aside before he did something really foolish like taking her in the elevator.

Ah, hell, he needed to get away from the office. To bring her to a place where they could work out the details of this relationship they were in. Because he'd realized as he'd seen her standing alone staring at pictures of his family that he wanted her by his side for the rest of his days.

He just didn't know how to keep her.

His hands were shaking and he felt like a weak man. What he felt for Holly was wildly different than anything he'd experienced before.

"What does this mean, Joe?" she asked.

Her lips were still red from his kiss, her lower lip a little swollen and her skin flushed with the first blush of sexual excitement. Concentrating on her words was hard, but he forced himself to do so, knowing that they needed to talk.

"It means so many things," he said, though he didn't feel confident to list them. He was more confident of Holly's reactions.

"That kiss felt like the beginning of something very hot and very carnal."

He gave her a wicked grin. "You do that to me. Will you come home with me, Holly?"

"For sex?" she asked, crossing her arms over her chest.

He tried to see this situation from her viewpoint but he couldn't. He was a man and he wanted her. But she was supposed to be the perceptive one. Women were supposed to understand feelings men had trouble vocalizing. Why wasn't she doing that? Why didn't she understand that it was a heck of a lot more than just sex when they were together?

"Stop saying 'sex' as if the physical act is all that's between us."

"Well, let's review the facts. Fact one—you didn't call me for two days. Fact two—as soon as we're together again you kiss me like you want a quickie in the elevator."

He clenched his hands. "I want a hell of a lot more than that. And I think you know it."

"I've given up second-guessing you, Joe. I'd have

wagered all the money I won in the Baronessa contest that you were going to call me. I don't understand anything about you.''

"Understand this. If I wanted sex I could have it with any number of women. But I've never wanted a cold act between two strangers. The other night when we *made love,* you touched my soul, woman.'' He took her face in his hands and kissed her with all the feelings in his soul and realized that if he had to let her go he'd be a shattered man.

She stared at him, her eyes wide and her mouth open the slightest bit. He knew she had to be mad because he hadn't called. But explanations would take time. And he didn't want to do that at work where his family could interrupt them at any moment.

"Please, come home with me," he said.

"Why?''

"I have things to say to you that I can only say there.''

She watched him, eyes questioning but burning with a hope that he felt in his soul. He wasn't sure how but he knew he'd fallen in love with her. The moment they'd met he'd known there was something special about her. Something that no other woman held. But it was two short nights ago, when she'd taken his hand and led him to her bedroom, that he'd realized she'd found the soft underbelly he'd always hidden.

Realized that this woman had the power to heal a

hurt he'd never known he'd been carrying with him. And that realization was the kind that crippled a man.

He didn't want to have to acknowledge that she'd become a part of him that he couldn't live without. Wasn't sure he was ready to let another woman past his defenses. Because if Mary's death had taught him one thing, it was that fate was fickle.

He realized he was holding his breath as he awaited Holly's answer. He looked at her beseechingly.

"Okay." It was all she said, but it was the word he was longing to hear.

He released the emergency-stop button and then pushed the lobby button. He held Holly's hand tightly in his, barely able to wait until the ride was over to get to his house.

"Do you want to leave your car here?" he asked.

"No, I'll follow you."

"I promise you won't regret it."

"Don't make promises you might not keep."

"I'm not."

He walked away and felt her gaze on him all the way to his car. His hands shook, and he realized that more than lust and love were riding him. There was also the very real fear that Holly might love him back.

Holly followed Joe to his house. His neighborhood was newer than hers and more exclusive, having a security guard at a gated entrance. The guard waved her through. Each house was beautiful, each yard neatly landscaped. From where she sat it looked like a perfect world—and one she could never fit into.

As she followed Joe's sedan she realized that their lives were worlds apart. She didn't see a way they could ever really be together.

Each of these houses probably cost five times hers. Aside from the financial aspects, her family needed her. She couldn't imagine Joe wanting to spend the night in her childhood bedroom, because her father couldn't be left alone at night.

Joe pulled into a three-car garage and Holly parked in the driveway. Joe walked toward her and opened her door. But she just sat there, staring up at him.

Whatever had happened in the elevator had freed him. It had almost paralyzed her when she realized she would have had sex with him again even though he'd avoided her for two days. Even though only an hour earlier she wasn't sure she'd ever hear from him again. It scared her to think he meant that much to her. And that her own self-esteem meant so little.

But Joe went to her head and her heart. From her past she'd learned that men like Roger would take from her whatever she was willing to give. But Joe was the first guy who cherished her. He'd sent her flowers and taken her to a romantic restaurant. He'd played basketball with her and let her see his vulnerable side.

"Holly?" His voice reached through her thoughts.

"I'm not sure why I'm here," she said.

"Because we need each other," he said.

"We do?"

He nodded. She climbed out of her car and before she could move, he picked her up and carried her toward his house.

"Why are you carrying me?" she asked. No man had ever carried her before. She clung to his shoulders and tried not to think about the fact that he was fulfilling her secret dreams.

"Because you need romance."

How did he know? It made her vulnerable to realize that he saw things she thought she'd hidden. That he didn't look at her and see a strong person who could support and shelter her family. That he might be the one man who saw straight to her soul. Because Joe wasn't the kind of man she could protect herself from. She'd become aware of that when she'd driven to his office.

"Do you need romance too?" she asked. She wanted to be his equal not the needy one.

"Oh, yeah."

She forgot about her worries as he carried her over the threshold of his house and set her on her feet. Fresh flowers sat in a vase on the table in his foyer. The marble entryway led to a grand staircase. She should be dressed to the nines instead of wearing a three-year-old sundress. "I wish I were wearing something more appropriate."

"I wish you were nude."

That surprised a chuckle out of her. "Joe."

"It's the truth, but I promised you we'd talk, so perhaps it's better you are clothed."

His place was professionally decorated, immaculately clean and, she saw as he flicked on the lights, very much like the man himself. At first glance the modern furniture with sleek lines appeared smooth and sophisticated. But the dark and disturbing realism in art showed the real man.

"Should I remove my shoes?"

"Only if you want to."

She slid out of them because, unless she was mistaken, he had Berber carpet and she loved the way it felt under her feet.

He led her into the living room. Through a wall of glass she saw a deck that overlooked a large swimming pool complete with a waterfall at one end.

"Please sit down," he said.

She seated herself on the love seat and watched Joe pace the room. Whatever he had to say he was nervous about it.

"I'm sorry I didn't call you," he began.

"Why didn't you?"

"When Mary died my life changed."

"What does that have to do with not calling me?"

"I'm not good with words. But I'll try to explain," he said.

"That's all I ask."

"I vowed to never again feel defenseless."

"In what way?"

"Emotionally. I'm not comfortable talking about

my feelings, Holly. So I'm not going to say this again.''

She went to him, put her arms around his broad shoulders. There was a part of Joe that he didn't want her to see but he showed her anyway. Despite her earlier accusation, she knew this man wasn't a coward.

''I'm afraid of love,'' he whispered against her hair.

She held him tighter. ''Why?''

''Because of the heartache it can bring.''

''Love doesn't always end that way.''

''In my experience it does.''

''I've never experienced love,'' Holly said at last.

''Why not?''

''I don't know. I think, like you, I've been afraid of it.''

''When I saw you waiting for me this afternoon…you seemed so brave and unafraid.''

''Don't let appearances fool you. I was shaking in my boots.''

''That's just it. You were scared but you'd come to find me. And I knew then I couldn't let you get away again.''

Holly's heart froze in her chest. What was he saying? Oh, God. She didn't want to hear whatever he planned to say next. He opened his mouth but she went up on tiptoe and covered his lips with hers.

Ten

Joe had always been the aggressor in all his relationships. That was what had enabled him to keep others at bay for so long. And not just in his relationships with the opposite sex. In all relationships he'd manipulated people in a way that allowed him to be comfortable.

With Holly it had been because she was as leery as he was and they both needed time to adjust.

He wanted to tell Holly how he felt about her but she'd kissed him in a way that made thinking stop and feeling begin. Two days had been too long. He wanted to take her to bed and keep her there until neither of them had any strength left.

"We'll talk more later," he said, lifting her off

her feet and carrying her upstairs to his bedroom. "It feels like it's been years since I buried myself in you."

She wrapped her arms around him and toyed with the hair at the back of his neck. "For me too."

There was something different about Holly. He couldn't put his finger on it but he'd figure it out. She whispered seductive promises in his ear as he carried her, and by the time he'd reached his bedroom he was rock hard and ready for her.

Unlike the rest of the house, his bedroom wasn't immaculate. A big-screen TV dominated one wall and his king-size bed the other.

He tossed her on the bed and followed her down, covering her body with his. But she stopped him, holding him at bay. "I'm in charge this time."

The thought brought him to his knees. He rolled onto his back and waited for her to make her move. She stood at the foot of the bed and removed her clothing with carefully measured movements. Her eyes never left his.

He reached for the buttons on his shirt but she shook her head. "Not yet, I'll get your clothes in a minute."

He propped two pillows behind his head and watched her through narrowed eyes as naked now, she removed his shoes and socks. Then she climbed up on the bed and unfastened his belt, tugging it free of his pants. She unbuttoned his shirt and pushed it down his arms. Joe flung it across the room.

She walked her fingers down his chest and then slid one under his waistband. He was so painfully hard now that he was afraid he'd come when she touched his zipper.

"Holly, no more. I need you now." He needed to bury himself in her again. He wanted to seal the two of them together so that nothing could come between them. Not fate, not family, not anything.

"Please, Joe. I want to make love to you."

He clenched his fists, reaching for the control he'd always had in the past. But everything was different with Holly. "I'll try."

"That's all I ask," she said, lowering his zipper and pushing his pants down his legs. He kicked his feet free of them and lay tensely waiting for her to make her next move. She took him in her slender hands, holding him carefully.

He had to touch her. He caressed the curve of her buttocks, the long line of her legs, the weight of her breasts. "I can't hold out much longer."

She gave him a seductive smile. "Waiting makes everything better."

"You've got thirty seconds, then I'm in charge."

"We'll see about that," she said, lowering her head and taking him in her mouth.

Everything inside him clenched. Just the sight of Holly with her red hair brushing his thighs and her mouth moving so passionatcly on him was enough to bring him to the edge. But he wasn't going over without her.

He tugged her up and over him, brought her mouth to his and tasted himself on her. She rocked against him, her humid warmth making him realize that he didn't have a condom. He almost didn't care.

He wanted to feel her naked flesh on his. Wanted to experience only Holly without any barriers. Not the ones in his heart or the ones on his body.

But he knew they weren't ready for the consequences that making love without a condom could bring. He stretched for the nightstand and opened the drawer.

"Let me," she said.

He didn't know if he'd be able to bear her hands on him again. He was so close to the edge. Only the look on her face as she tore open the packet and covered him in one long caress made it possible for him to wait. "Come here, Holly."

He pulled her over him, held her hips firmly and thrust up into her. She threw her head back and gripped his shoulders. Her nails bit into his flesh in a way that made him feel good. Something more than a physical act was taking place between them.

He lifted his head and took her nipple in his mouth, teasing her with his tongue and then suckling deeply. She moaned and started rocking faster against him. Using his grip on her hips, he slowed the pace. Now that he was inside her he wanted to take his time. He needed to drive them both crazy with wanting before they reached the ultimate satisfaction.

"Joe, hurry," she said.

"Uh-uh, now I'm in charge," he said with a wicked grin.

Leaning forward, she found the pulse beating at the base of his neck with her mouth. She suckled strongly and he felt his control snap. His grip on her hips changed. He thrust heavily into her. Once and then twice. She called his name and he felt her body tightening rhythmically around his. He thrust into her one more time and let his orgasm wash over him.

Holly collapsed on his chest and he held her tightly to him, knowing he'd never let her go.

She had to go.

That was Holly's first awareness when she woke in Joe's bed the next morning. Careful not to disturb him, she dressed quickly while he slept and left. It scared her—how much he was coming to mean to her. She wasn't ready for that kind of all-consuming relationship in her life.

The bakery was busy, so Holly didn't pay any attention when Colleen, the manager, entered the kitchen. "There's a man here to see you."

"Who?" she asked. It was busier than usual for a Friday, thanks to a feature in the *Boston Globe* food section this week. More people were here to sample their pastries.

"I don't know. He's tall, dark and Italian."

Joe. "Tell him I'm busy."

"Too late," Joe said from the doorway.

"I really can't talk right now, Joe."

"Then listen."

She glanced warily at him. Colleen left the kitchen and Holly slid the tray of cream puffs into the oven and returned to the counter where she was in the process of frosting a wedding cake.

"Can I call you later?" Holly asked. She didn't like to have different areas of her world colliding. Joe belonged to her and her alone. Now that he'd been here Colleen would want to talk about him. Then, when he didn't want to see her anymore, Colleen would want to analyze it. Holly preferred to keep her relationships to herself.

He moved toward her. Darn it. He'd obviously come from the office and she wished he looked stuffy in a business suit instead of handsome and sexy. Seeing him so neat and put together made her remember what he'd looked like underneath her last night, his face flushed with desire and his body ready for hers.

Joe shook his head. "I'd say yes but I get the feeling you're avoiding me. I thought you'd forgiven me for not calling."

"I did."

"Then what's up?"

"I'm at work, Joe."

"I know. Can't you take a break for ten minutes? We can go out back and talk."

Holly checked the timer on the cream puffs and looked at the cake. "I've only got five minutes."

"I'll take it."

She led the way out the back door to the battered picnic table in the alley that she and Colleen sometimes ate lunch at. A warm afternoon breeze blew through the alleyway, stirring the hair at the back of her neck.

Joe gave her a light kiss and pulled back quickly. "There's a lot I have to say to you, Holly, but this isn't the place for it."

"I know. I'm sorry we're so crazy here today," she said. Joe looked like a man with a mission and it scared her to think she might be what he was focusing on. He had an intensity that frightened her sometimes.

"Will you have dinner with me tonight?" he asked, holding her hand lightly in his. He traced the pattern of her freckles up her arm until they disappeared under her sleeve. His touch made her shiver and everything feminine in her clenched and softened.

She wanted to. But she was afraid of the emotion she saw in his eyes. She didn't want to know how he felt or hear things that would tempt her to break her commitment to her family. "I can't. My brothers are all going out and I promised my dad I'd stay with him."

His dark-chocolate gaze met hers. "I'd love to meet your dad."

For all his money, Joe was a very basic guy, and her dad and brothers would like him. Too bad they could never meet. "I don't think that's a good idea."

"Why not? You've met my family," he said.

She didn't want to tell him the truth. That she didn't want him to meet her family because once he did then she might have to choose between them. A lover demanded a few hours of her time, but a man who'd met the family, who wanted to spend the evening with her and her dad, that was a man who'd want more than late-night hours. And she didn't have that to give.

She gave him a stock reply. "Dad can be surly and he hasn't been feeling well. Maybe another time."

He watched her and she felt as if he could see past her half truth to the heart of the matter. She was tempted to hold her breath until he said, "If you're sure."

"I am." She forced a tight smile and changed the subject. "Isn't tomorrow your family's big reunion?"

"Yes. Will you come with me? The picnic will be a lot of fun and I'm sure we can avoid the press."

"Why do you want me to come?" she asked.

"You're important to me, Holly."

"It scares me to hear you say that," she admitted. It also made her heart fill with those impossible dreams she'd been having since he'd taken her to his house and let her make love to him. She'd never touched a man the way she'd touched Joe. Never felt so close to another person and never wanted to share her burdens with another person. Until Joe.

"Why?" he asked.

"I can't talk about it now. I've got to get back to work." Besides, before she explained her feelings to him, she had to work them out for herself.

"Will you go with me tomorrow?" he asked.

She wanted to spend the day with him. To meet his family again and see Joe in the environment where he was most at ease. One last day, she thought, then she'd break it off with him. "Yes. I'd like that."

"Good. I'll pick you up in the morning. It's an all-day thing with fireworks after dark."

"Okay," she said.

She started back toward the kitchen.

"Holly?"

"Yes."

"I know you're running. And eventually I'm going to catch you."

The family picnic was held at his parents' town house in Beacon Hill. Joe always loved going to his folks' place especially when the family was all there. Last night, sitting in his empty house alone, he'd realized what Holly needed to stop running from him. She needed him to make a commitment to her. In the beginning he'd been the aloof one and Holly the outgoing one. Now, however, she kept a part of herself walled off from him. A part of her that was very soft and very vulnerable.

But after today neither of them would have to be

alone any longer. Because today he planned to ask Holly to marry him.

After leaving her at the bakery yesterday afternoon, he'd realized that he had to show Holly that he regretted not calling her and that he meant for her place in his life to be a permanent one. He'd gone to the jewelry store and purchased a marquise-cut engagement ring for her.

He glanced into the rearview mirror for a glimpse in the back seat. It contained a change of clothes, which he'd no doubt need after the annual male versus female volleyball game. More important, it contained the ring.

Holly was waiting on the porch when he pulled up in front of her house. She wore khaki shorts cut high on her thigh, a slim-fitting sleeveless white shirt and deck shoes. She took his breath away. It amazed him to think that she was his woman.

She walked toward the car and he got out to open the door for her. She smiled when she saw him but she seemed tired and tense.

"Is your dad okay?"

"Yes, he's fine."

He took her in his arms and kissed her the way he'd wanted to yesterday at the bakery. She rose on tiptoe, wrapping her slender arms around him and holding him tightly to her. "Damn, I wish we could skip this thing and spend the day here in your bed."

"We can't?"

"No. This is a command performance for the

press. All Barones must be present and accounted for.''

"Flint and Gina again?''

"Yes,'' Joe said with a wry grin.

"Well, then, let's get going. I'd hate for you to get in trouble.''

"My folks have a spa tub at their place. Why don't you bring your swimsuit and a change of clothes.''

Holly ran inside and was back out in a flash. The drive to his parents' place went quickly, but as they neared the house, traffic became heavy and Joe knew from the past that parking would be hard to find.

"Do you mind walking from here? It's about three blocks.''

"No. It's a nice day.''

"Good. It'll give us time to talk.''

"Okay,'' she said.

Joe parked the car and they both got out. Holly carried her straw beach bag and Joe his duffel. He put his free arm around her waist and kept his pace shorter to match hers. It was the first time in a long time that he felt at peace with himself and the world around him. He saw the beauty of the summer day and the beauty of life with Holly by his side.

"I've been thinking about our relationship,'' she said.

"Me too.''

"I wasn't expecting you, Joe.''

He smiled down at her. "Me neither, but I'm glad I found you, Holly.''

"Really?"

This woman needed to realize her own importance to those around her. She was so giving and caring, he doubted she understood how deeply she affected the people she interacted with. "Really."

He dropped a kiss on her lips.

"Hey, Joe."

He turned to see Nick standing behind him, carrying two bags. His eldest brother looked happier than Joe could remember seeing him in years. But then the love of a good woman could do that to a man.

"Nick, this is Holly Fitzgerald. Holly, this is my oldest brother, Nick."

"Nice to meet you," Holly said.

"The pleasure's all mine. I'd stay and chat, but I've got to get this ice to Dad," Nick said.

"We ran out already?" Joe asked. His father was meticulous in the planning of the family reunion.

"No, there was an accident with one of the coolers, so we needed a few more bags."

"Where's Gail?" Joe asked, looking for his brother's wife.

"With the women, planning volleyball strategy."

"Oh, they think they can win this year?"

"I believe so," Nick said as he disappeared around the corner of the house. "What's this about volleyball?" Holly asked Joe.

"We have an annual grudge match, boys versus girls."

"Who's ahead?"

"We're tied but the boys won last year."

"Should be interesting," Holly said.

"It should be. Come on, let me introduce you to everybody." Joe deposited their bags on the patio and put his arm around Holly. He'd been alone so long that he'd forgotten how good it felt to have someone special by his side.

His cousin Daniel was here and brought his friend Ashraf ibn-Saalem. Holly waited until they moved away from the friends before she said, "Ash looks strong. The boys might have an unfair advantage if he plays."

"Reese and Alex are both not here this year, so Ash will even the playing field. Besides, the girls have Gail on their team."

"Listen to you. Is she their secret weapon?"

"She might be. She plays on a coed team. Besides, the women in this family are tricky."

"Watch it, Joe. Mom might hear you," Gina said from behind them. She smiled a greeting at Holly. "Hello, Holly. Want to help us teach the Barone men a lesson?"

Holly returned the smile. "I might enjoy that."

Joe groaned. "Is Flint playing?"

"I don't think so. He's got the press to wrangle with."

"Why aren't you with the press?" Joe asked.

"Who'd give you a hard time if it wasn't me?" Gina asked with a smile.

Joe turned toward Holly. "Hey, help me out here."

"I think you're doing fine," she said, laughing up at him.

Joe looked at her and felt a confidence he hadn't felt in a long time. He was in love with Holly Fitzgerald and he couldn't wait to make her his wife.

Eleven

Holly, at Gina's urging, joined the women's team for the volleyball match. Joe was sexier than any man ought to be in gym shorts and no shirt. His chest muscles rippled as he tossed the ball in the air before the game began and caught it. It was a hot late-July day and most of the women wore bikini tops and shorts, Holly included.

On the sidelines cheering the teams on was Alex Barone's new wife, Daisy, with her new baby, Angel. Everyone knew the baby's biological father wasn't Alex, but he was the only daddy Angel would know. And it was clear from what Holly had heard that Alex adored his daughter and his wife.

The baby was so cute that Holly had been tempted

to ask to hold her. But this wasn't her family so she'd watched from the sidelines, feeling a heaviness in her heart that this clan wasn't her own.

Though there was a good deal of ribbing, it was clear this year the Barone women weren't going home losers. Joe huddled close with the men's team, and as Holly watched him, she understood the missing piece of the puzzle he was to her.

Seeing him with his family, watching him move and interact with them, made one thing crystal clear: Joe wasn't meant to be a single guy. He was meant to be a family man. He played with Nicholas's toddler daughter, Molly, as if she was his own.

Did Joe want kids? Despite the closeness they shared, she knew little of his dreams for the future. Holly was amazed. For the first time she actually wanted to think about a future with a man.

Though there were eight kids and four cousins, the Barones were a tight-knit clan. She suddenly wanted to learn more about them all.

"You all are descended from two Barone brothers?" Holly asked Gina right before the game started.

"My uncle Paul is a twin. When they were two days old, Uncle Luke was abducted and never found. The family was shaken by that," Gina said.

"How horrible for your family."

"It was. But that was a long time ago." After a few minutes, Gina remarked, "Joe seems happy today."

Holly wasn't sure she wanted to have this conversation. She wasn't sure she herself knew what was going on with Joe. "Yes, he does."

Gina said nothing for a few minutes, watching her family and friends mill around the backyard. "It's about time."

Holly didn't want her to have the wrong impression. "Gina, we— Things aren't— Look, your brother and I are just friends."

Gina put her hand on Holly's arm. "I think friends is a good place to start."

Holly felt tears sting the back of her eyes. She'd always wanted sisters just to even the score in her family, but now she realized what she'd missed. Holly stood at the sidelines, watching the Barones interact, feeling a keen sense of longing that she'd never felt before.

Though her family was close, that closeness was tinged by a sense of duty and obligation. She'd promised her mother that she'd take care of the boys and keep the family together. She'd never really felt comfortable relaxing around her family the way she did here today with the Barones.

"Ready to get your butt kicked?" Joe asked, coming up and putting his arms around her. Most of the Barones were taking a last-minute break before the game started. Carlo and Moira, Joe's parents, had chairs set up on either side of the court, and those who weren't playing were on the sidelines already.

"Hardly. According to Gina, the men are better at fireworks than volleyball."

"Really?" he asked, running his finger down the side of her face. She shivered as awareness lit a fire that ended in the pit of her belly.

"Yup," she said, giving in to the urge to caress his stomach. His muscles rippled in response and his eyes narrowed. She recognized the gleam in them as a purely sexual one.

"I beg to differ. Fireworks are all flash."

Joe was different today. Lighter somehow. No longer aloof and brooding but almost happy. It scared her to think she might be responsible for the change because that meant she'd have to be responsible for keeping him happy and she didn't know if she could do it. She had enough to worry about with Dad's health and her brothers' lives.

"Are you trying to say there's more than flash to you?" she asked, still teasing him. He'd pulled her more fully against him so that only an inch of space separated their bodies. She could scarcely breathe as she stood there wishing they were in a private place so she could caress him as she longed to. Why had she decided to turn him down for dinner last night?

The reasons, which had seemed so relevant yesterday, paled as she stood trembling in his arms. Joe tilted her head back with his hand, and as she gazed up at him she felt her heart lurch. She realized in that moment that she loved him. Loved his tough-as-nails side, loved his soft side where his family was concerned and most especially loved the way he made her feel—as if she was the most beautiful woman on earth.

"I think you know there is," he said softly.

Bracing her hands on his shoulders, she stood on tiptoe so their lips were only a breath apart. "Maybe."

He brushed his lips against hers and then pulled back. "Maybe?"

She just raised one eyebrow at him.

"What do you think of this?"

He bent his head and kissed her in a way that left no doubt there was something very solid about Joe Barone. And that he wasn't just a quick burst of bright lights.

Catcalls and whistles broke through the spell Joe was effortlessly weaving around her. He pulled back and gave her a tight hug before walking toward the men's team. Holly went to join the women, feeling more dazed and confused than she ever had before. Something magical had taken shape between them. But could magic last the rigors of her everyday life?

As the sun began to set, Joe took the ring he'd purchased for Holly from his gym bag and went searching for her. His sister Maria had gotten sick during the volleyball game and was now sitting on a lounge chair with a cup of Sprite. She seemed a little pale to Joe, but his sister Rita, who was a nurse, ruled the episode as heat exhaustion.

Even without Maria's help the women had beaten

the men in the first match. The second match, the men had come back. The tie breaking game had been when Maria had gotten sick, but even without her, the women had beaten the men, making them the new Barone family volleyball champions. The women had done their victory dance and earned bragging rights for the coming year.

But there was only one woman he was interested in now. Where was Holly? Joe started toward his brother Nick to ask him if he'd seen her, but then realized Nick and his cousin Derrick were having a heated discussion. He turned instead to the cluster of women by the food table.

"Have you seen Holly?" he asked his mom.

"No, dear, I haven't. But I meant to tell you, I really like her," she said.

"Me too," said Emily, his cousin. She'd been going through a rough spot, having amnesia and witnessing the fire that had been started at the Baronessa factory. But being outside today with her fiancé, Shane, she seemed happy. Shane had been a great addition to the Barone men's team.

"She's not like Mary," his mom added.

His mother was right. Mary had always been fragile, never able to participate in any of the family activities. She was always on the sidelines, watching, while Holly was in the middle of the action, a part of the group.

"Dad's looking for you, Joe. You're needed at the fireworks bunker," said Gina.

"If you see Holly, tell her I need to talk to her."

"I will," his mom said.

Joe joined his father, uncle Paul, his brothers and male cousins at the fireworks bunker. They worked quickly to set the fuses and ready the explosives for the annual display. The new men in the family were there too, fitting easily into the group of joking men.

Joe worked at his father's side, realizing that he wanted a son to pass on this tradition to. He wanted to share his family's customs with his kids and make sure they took pride in them and passed them on to their kids.

It was a humbling moment. He hadn't thought about the future in so long that he'd been locked in the present. Asking Holly to marry him today wasn't just something he was doing for himself and Holly. It was something he was doing for his family.

When everything was set, he headed back toward the house and found Holly standing with the women. He took her hand and led her away from everyone. He found a bench nestled in the corner of his mother's garden. Carefully, he seated Holly on the bench and sat down next to her.

"Did you have fun today?" he asked. He wanted to make sure his family hadn't overwhelmed her.

"I did. Your family is wonderful," she said.

"They are. I have something important to say to you, Holly."

She tilted her head to look at him. Her eyes were dreamy. "What?"

Wrapping his arms around her, he took a deep breath. Now that she was in his arms, all the vulnerabilities he had came rushing back. Love was a risk he'd fought taking for a long time.

But this was Holly. The woman who'd freed him from the deep, frozen place his life had become. The woman who'd lit a fire in his blood and sent those flames through his soul. The woman who'd made him realize he wanted to dream again.

"I love you," he whispered against the top of her head.

He felt her shudder. She pulled back and looked up at him, her eyes wide with fear and something else. A knot formed in the pit of his stomach.

She was probably worried that he wasn't ready to make a commitment to her. He eased off the bench and went down on one knee, fumbling in his pocket for the ring.

She started to speak, but he covered her lips with his hand. "Part of me died with Mary, Holly. And I thought I'd never find a reason to love again. But you showed me what I'd been missing. You made me realize how lonely life was."

She reached out and cupped his jaw. "You weren't lonely. You had your family."

"You're right, I did. But I needed more."

"What did you need?" she asked.

"I needed you. Holly, will you marry me?"

Holly gulped and fought back tears. He *loved* her. No one had said those words to her since her mother died. And never had she needed to hear them as much as she did now.

She couldn't control the thrill that speared through her or the sudden tightness in her throat. These twin responses made it impossible for her to speak for a few minutes.

This was the one thing she wanted and dreaded. She couldn't marry Joe. Couldn't possibly become Mrs. Joe Barone because he didn't know the real Holly. He'd never even met her family. And her family was her first duty. A long time ago she'd made promises at her mother's deathbed that she'd make sure the Fitzgeralds were always together. They needed her 24/7, and if she lived up to that commitment to them, she couldn't take another vow with Joe.

She didn't realize she was crying until she felt the moisture on her face. She pulled her hands from his and wiped her cheeks. She didn't face the other truth that lay beneath her obligation to her family. Joe made her feel emotions that were uncomfortable. They were the extremes of her soul. He made her want to be daring in ways she'd never anticipated.

"Joe, I..."

Suddenly she couldn't do it. She couldn't sit here and tell him no in front of his family. But marrying him would be a mistake, for both of them, she wasn't going to make.

"I'm sorry," she said. She stood and ran from him as if demons were chasing her.

She reached the street and realized she had no way of getting home. She'd ridden to the picnic with Joe. She took her cell phone from her pocket and called her eldest brother, Clint. He promised to come and get her. But she had to hang out for fifteen minutes.

Joe didn't follow her and she didn't blame him. What kind of woman had soul-sex with a man then turned him down when he asked her to marry him? She didn't like the answers she found deep inside. She sat on the stoop waiting for Clint, wondering if she'd ever really be able to share her life with anyone.

More important, she wondered if she'd ever come to terms with her hang-ups. Because the real reason she'd run away from Joe wasn't her family. The real reason was that she knew life was fragile. She knew how quickly and how unfairly fate could change. One minute you were the cherished daughter of a happily married couple, the next minute you were the only woman in your family and had enormous responsibilities.

"Holly?"

She glanced over her shoulder at Joe, standing in the front doorway of his parents' house. He was backlit by the wall sconces in the foyer, making it impossible to see his expression. Life had dealt Joe enough heartache, she thought. He shouldn't have fallen in love with her.

"I'm sorry," she said again. She didn't know what else to say. She hadn't expected love. It seemed this relationship of theirs had started out as a one-night stand but then turned into something she still couldn't define.

"Is this anything we can work out?" he asked.

She wished. But asking him to wait a few years for her didn't seem like much of a solution. "I don't think so."

"Is it me?" he asked at last.

"Oh, Joe. No, it's not you." She laced her fingers together to keep from reaching out for him.

"Holly, I'm trying to be patient and understanding—two things I'm not known for."

"I appreciate it." She wished her brother would show up. She didn't like the direction this conversation was going.

"Then give me some explanations," he said.

"Listen, my family needs me. I'm the glue that holds them together. I can't walk away from that."

He sighed and rubbed his jaw. "Believe it or not, I wasn't asking you to cut off your relationship with them."

"I know. Only it's a full-time job. I have to spend the night at my dad's house occasionally. I have to finish paying for Brian's last year of college. I have to—"

"You don't have to do that stuff."

"If I don't, who will?"

"Those brothers of yours aren't children anymore. They can take care of themselves."

"I know they aren't babies."

"Then why do you insist on treating them like they are?" he asked.

"I don't."

"You do and I think I know why."

"What makes you such an expert on my life?"

He narrowed his gaze on her and she shivered under the intensity there. "I know you intimately, Holly. I think that counts for something."

"Physical knowledge doesn't give you any insight."

"The hell it doesn't. You don't share yourself easily and you're crazy if you think I don't know it."

She hugged herself to keep from exploding into a million pieces. But didn't say anything, only waited to hear what else he thought he knew about her.

"You accused me once of being a coward. I just realized that I wasn't the only one who was running away."

"I'm not."

"You are. You're afraid to let yourself be happy."

"What makes you so confident you make me happy?"

"I'm not—at least not anymore."

Clint pulled to a stop at the curb and honked the horn. "That's my brother."

"Go ahead, run, I'm not stopping you. But if you decide you're tired of playing the martyr, give me a call."

Joe walked inside without another word. The sound of the door closing echoed in her heart and she knew she'd just thrown away her chance at happily-ever-after.

Twelve

Holly hadn't been able to sleep in her bed last night or on the couch. The memories of Joe were still too strong. So she'd grabbed the quilt she and her mother had made when Holly was thirteen, wrapped herself in that and slept in the Kennedy rocker on the back porch.

Sleep, she decided, was highly overrated.

Holly had always wanted to think of herself as daring, as taking risks that seemed to be exciting. But only yesterday, when she'd heard Joe ask her to marry him, did she realize that all those risks had been superficial.

When the time came for her to really put herself on the line, she'd ducked and run for cover. And she'd hurt the one man who'd made her feel like a woman. The one man who'd always treated her as if he cherished her. The one man who'd proven to be her Prince Charming.

The doorbell rang and Holly ignored it. There wasn't anyone she wanted to see this morning. Especially not one of her nosey neighbors.

"Holly, you home?" It was her father.

Darn it, he had a key. She pushed herself off the rocker and entered her house. Her dad and brothers dominated the small entryway. They all held something, her dad a carafe, which she knew would have coffee in it, Matt held the newspaper, Brian had a bag from Kirkpatrick's Bakery and Clint held a jug of orange juice.

She was touched. They'd brought her breakfast. They never had before. She blinked back tears. Hell, she was getting too emotional lately. Maybe her period was going to start soon. Or maybe she'd finally had her emotional gates battered down by a certain Italian and maybe, she thought, they weren't going back into place so easily.

"Morning, guys," she said.

She hugged her dad and brothers and they all settled at her kitchen table. In the middle of the table was the vase with the flowers Joe had sent.

The blooms were still flourishing, and seeing them made her feel like a big coward. Joe had lost way more than she ever had and yet he was willing to risk the pain of rejection again. Something she couldn't do. Even now, as much as she wanted to go to him, something kept her from doing it.

Something more than her family.

"What are you doing here this morning?" she asked, needing to forget about Joe and romantic gestures. She took the vase and moved it to the counter behind the canisters, out of her view.

"Have you seen the newspaper?" Clint asked. He took mugs from the rack on the wall and handed them around the table before filling each cup with the strong brew. Matt leaned back on his chair and opened the refrigerator and took out the milk.

Her brothers were tall and lean with auburn hair that they'd all inherited from their dad. Clint, the tallest, worked at a computer gaming company and seldom wore anything other than T-shirts with graphic designs and board shots. Matt was a bartender and wore a uniform of black T-shirts that molded to his chest and tight-fitting jeans because he said the ladies like his butt. Brian had a part-time entry-level job in an insurance company and wore button down shirts and chinos.

"No. I haven't. Is that why you all are here?"

No one said anything. Matt passed the paper to her. Holly just looked at it. The headlines hardly ever changed anymore.

"Check out page two."

She flipped it open and there was a picture of her and Joe at the picnic. She knew when it had been taken. Right before that damn volleyball game. She remembered the look on his face as he'd lowered his head to hers.

"Who is this guy, Holly?" Matt asked.

"Why haven't we met him?" Brian asked.

"Joe Barone. And because I don't have time for a serious relationship."

"These eyes might be old but that picture looks pretty serious to me," her dad, Dave, said.

She didn't realize how they'd appeared to anyone looking on. Joe was going to have to face the same questions from his family today. Did any of them know he'd proposed last night? Had any of the Barones seen them tucked away in his mom's garden?

Oh, God, she hoped not. Because after her conversation with Gina, she had a feeling the entire Barone clan might come after her when they realized how badly she'd hurt one of their own. "It's not serious anymore, Dad."

"Why not?" he asked.

Holly shrugged. The truth was hard to explain, especially since she knew she'd have to admit she was a chicken. "Because I still have commitments to you all and I can't give myself to him only halfway."

"Who asked you to?" her dad asked.

"Dad, you know I need to be available to you guys."

"Sweetheart, we're a family. That means we take care of each other."

She stared at her father and brothers stubbornly. She knew her job. They weren't the ones Mom had pulled close right before she'd died. They weren't the ones Mom had made promise to nurture and protect the family. They weren't the ones who'd ever noticed that without her the family would fall apart.

Her dad took a deep breath. "In that case, then, you're fired."

"What are you talking about?" Holly asked.

"Just what the old man said. You don't have to take care of us anymore," Matt said.

"Why not?"

Brian took her hand in his. "We grew up, Holly. Your job is done."

"What about Dad?" she asked. He was the one that she worried about. He needed someone to watch over him.

"What about me?" her dad asked.

"You're still not healthy," Holly said.

"There's no reason I can't be if I just follow the doctor's orders."

"But you never do," Holly said.

"Maybe it's time I did."

"Are you guys serious?" she asked at last.

"Yes." Clint spoke for them.

Everyone was quiet for a few minutes. Holly took a sip of her coffee, realizing that her family had given her the green light to go after Joe if she wanted to. Oh yeah, she wanted to. But would he take her back?

She'd have to take a big risk. She'd have to show him that her love for him was as deep as his was. He'd made a grand gesture—giving her the romance he thought she needed. Only, he needed the romance too.

"I hope we're going to get to meet this Joe Barone."

"Oh, Dad. I hope so too. But I hurt him pretty bad."

"How are you going to make it right?" Clint asked.

"I don't know."

She finished breakfast with her brothers and father. They talked about going fishing later. Holly tried to pay attention, but one thought kept rolling through her head. How was she going to convince Joe that she loved him and was ready to make a lifetime commitment to him?

Joe had made some bad choices in his life. Coming to dinner at his folks' the night after Holly turned down his proposal probably ranked up in the top three. But he'd felt that family guilt again, and his mom wouldn't take no for an answer.

He left their house and drove slowly back through the city. Boston at night was one of his favorite sights. It was still as busy and active as Boston during the day, only at night it seemed cleaner somehow, more mysterious. And he was the first to admit he loved a good mystery.

He also admitted to himself that Holly was still a mystery, which was probably why she'd turned him down. He'd asked only one other woman to marry him. He wasn't the type of person who gave himself easily, and it bothered him that she'd not given herself to him with the same depth.

His house was big and lonely and he didn't want to go back there without Holly. He didn't want to sleep in his king-size bed and feel that it was too big because there wasn't a tiny redhead nestled next to him on the mattress.

He'd slept in one of the guest bedrooms last night. The same one he'd used for six months after Mary had died. It was a sparsely decorated room with a narrow single bed and no memories. To be honest, he'd never thought to sleep in that room again. He'd put that part of his life behind him. Learned a hard lesson about caring. Apparently he wasn't as quick as he'd always thought, because Holly's rejection had caught him by surprise.

He'd hedged his bets by proposing to her with his family surrounding him. He'd counted on her caring for him enough to say yes while his family was close by. But he'd forgotten that Holly was a sassy woman and not one who made decisions easily.

Aside from the timing, which he thought most women would find romantic, he didn't regret asking her to marry him. His love for Holly had come unexpectedly. It seemed to him a man shouldn't have more than one shot at the brass ring. But having been given that second chance, he'd known better than to let it pass him by.

No, he didn't regret asking her to marry him. He

just wished he'd understood better why she'd turned him down. But he refused to spend any more time thinking about it. He was going home, getting drunk, and on Monday he'd worry about it again.

Maybe after he'd drunk the better part of a fifth of scotch he'd be able to sleep or at least pass out so that he wouldn't have to spend the long, lonely hours between now and dawn replaying every moment he'd spent with Holly.

He pulled into his subdivision and drove to his house. It was dark, with only the automatic landscape lights illuminating it. Sitting there, he let the car idle and he worried that his life was becoming like this house. Nice on the outside…empty on the inside.

He drove into his garage and parked the car. No more thinking. He went to his bedroom and changed into a pair of low-slung jeans. With his chest and feet bare, he entered the wet-bar area of the living room and snagged a bottle of single malt scotch that he'd picked up last summer when he'd visited Scotland with his oldest brother.

He grabbed a highball glass and tossed some ice cubes in it. Just because he was drinking didn't mean he had to go totally low-class. His mother had raised him to be a gentleman. Even when he planned to get sloshed, he hung on to that thought.

Not that his manners had impressed Holly.

He poured the liquor into his glass and walked out onto the deck. The night sky was full of stars, and the smell of jasmine filled the air. As he lowered himself to the hardwood lounger, he wondered why life would give him two women to love and not let him keep either.

He took a swallow of scotch. He wasn't a self-pitying guy, so he wasn't about to go down that road. But it pissed the hell out of him every time he remembered the last sight of Holly. Arms around her waist, tears gleaming in her eyes. Sure made a man feel like a bastard to make a woman cry.

He took another swallow from his glass. This looked like an all-night project, which was okay with him because he had the time. In fact, he had nothing but time looming in front of him.

The doorbell rang when he was about halfway through the bottle. He ignored the first summons, feeling the effects of the booze and not wanting to have to be sociable with anyone.

The doorbell rang again, this time a continuous ringing as if the person on the other side was not lifting his finger off the buzzer.

It had to be a family member—probably Nick or Gina or one of his other siblings who continued to fall in love around him. They paired up like animals on Noah's ark, making him feel like a damn unicorn, not making the trip. He walked through the house.

"Go away," he growled through the door.

"No."

It sounded like Holly but he knew it couldn't be. He'd said unforgivable things to her. Called her a coward and a martyr. And if she was on the other side of the door he wasn't sure what to do.

The liquor bottle was still in his hand. He took a quick swig and then opened the door. She stood in front of him, looking like temptation. Like the woman he'd thought he'd come to know but with something more. Her eyes were clear and met his gaze, and she seemed nervous.

"What are you doing here?"

"You told me when I was tired of running to come and find you."

"Hell, Holly, I'm not at my best tonight."

"That's okay. I am."

She pushed against his chest. Her small hand was cool on his skin. He resisted for the simple reason that he wanted to enjoy her touch a little longer.

She flexed her fingers, her sharp nails biting the slightest bit. Lust settled low in his body and he almost grabbed her, tossed her over his shoulder and carried her to his bedroom.

But he'd told her he loved her and she'd walked away.

"Can I come in?" she asked.

He shrugged and backed up, letting her enter the house. She noticed the bottle of scotch in his hand and reached out to take it.

He lifted it out of her reach.

"Give me the bottle, Joe."

"I'm not done yet."

"Yes, you are," she said firmly. He'd never noticed that bossy tendency of hers before now. He had noticed her hair all red and pretty, falling around her shoulders. He wanted to feel it in his hands again. As he reached for her, Holly snagged the bottle.

Joe didn't let go at first, not sure he wanted to get rid of his only barrier. She tugged on it until he lost his grip, and some of the scotch sloshed over the side, splattering her hand and light raincoat.

"Damn," he said.

"How much have you drunk?" she asked.

"Not nearly as much as I plan to," he said, smiling at her.

She wiped her hand on her coat, then put her hands on her waist. Why was she here?

He needed his wits. He padded silently back out to the deck. There might be some more scotch in his glass. Vaguely he was aware of Holly following him.

Had he conjured her up by thinking about her? He'd planned to not think about her. He had a nice buzz going and all this thinking was messing with it.

He sank back to his chair, resting his elbows on his knees. Holly sat next to him, perched there gingerly as if afraid to relax.

Why was she here? This proved his father's point that a man should never drink too much. He rubbed his eyes with the heels of his hands. Maybe he'd imagined the entire episode and she wasn't really here.

Except he could smell. Damn, she smelled all sweet and sexy. He turned his head to the right and there she was. Sitting quietly, looking too damn beautiful with only the pool lights and the moon illuminating her. Hell, she always looked too good for him. Maybe she'd known all along that he wasn't the man for her.

"Why are you here?" he asked, his voice gruff.

"I..." She stood up, her long legs bare under the khaki-colored raincoat she had on. Her feet were shod in a pair of impossibly high stiletto heels. He had a lurid vision of her in nothing but the heels.

He squeezed his eyes shut, then he opened them again and realized it wasn't a vision. Holly had dropped the coat and stood in front of him clad only in her gorgeous freckles and those made-for-sex heels.

He couldn't think or speak. He rose in one fluid motion and staggered a bit. He wished he could be suddenly sober. But he couldn't. The least he could do was not take advantage of her, though if she stayed naked another minute he would. He picked her coat up and wrapped it around her.

"Holly—"

"I wanted to be as vulnerable as you were, Joe, when I said what I have to say."

Until that moment he hadn't realized she'd known the extent of his vulnerabilities. Until that moment he'd felt he'd retained a modicum of dignity. Until that moment he'd never realized how much he still loved her and that the anger in his heart wasn't true anger but a disguise of heartbreak so deep that he didn't know if he'd ever recover.

"I'm sorry," she said.

"I don't want your pity," he replied, realizing the words for truth. He wanted her back in his life but definitely not because she felt sorry for him.

"No, I didn't mean it like that. I apologize that I wasn't ready to be your wife when you offered me your heart," she said.

He shook his head trying to clear it. If he had half a brain, he'd go inside and make some coffee. "Why weren't you ready?"

"I don't know. I think you pegged it, though, when you said I was playing the martyr." She toyed with the strap on her raincoat, and he knew she was nervous. Hell, this was a mess. He'd never meant to hurt her.

"I was acting out."

"You were justified."

"Holly, why are you here?" he asked again.

"Would you sit down, please?"

He lowered himself to the lounger again. She shrugged out of her raincoat, laid it on the ground in front of his feet and then knelt on it.

He couldn't think with her naked at his feet. The alcohol he'd drunk earlier seemed to leave his system, replaced by desire. His blood rushed in his ears.

She took his hand in hers and looked up at him with sincerity in her eyes, and in the back of his mind he thought this was a good sign.

"Joseph Barone, you gave me a priceless gift and I wasn't worthy of it. But I ask you to reconsider." She smiled at him tentatively. "I love you," she said, tears in her eyes.

He reached out to cup her face in his hands. "I love you too," he said at last.

"I… Will you marry me?" she asked, holding up a small jewelry box.

"Hell, yes." He scooped her off her feet and carried her into the house.

She wrapped her arms around his neck as he bounded up the steps, then laid her on the center of his bed. He pushed off his jeans and briefs in one quick moment, then moved to cover her.

"Don't you want to know what changed my mind?" she asked, wrapping her arms around his shoulders.

"Later," he said, testing her and finding her wet and ready for his possession.

He thrust into her body, slid his arms up under her legs, folding them gently back toward her body. She moaned a deep husky sound that he'd die remembering and met him thrust for thrust.

Only when they were both shuddering with completion could he begin to think about their future. He knew he wasn't going to be able to wait long for a wedding.

He rolled off of her and cuddled her against him. "I'm never letting you go."

"Me neither," she said.

"I want to get married right away." Life had taught him to grasp the things he wanted and hold them close.

She nodded. "My dad and brothers have to be there."

"I want to meet them."

"They want to meet you too. I'm sorry I kept you from knowing them. I was afraid I couldn't have you and them."

"Why?"

"Love is a huge responsibility."

"Not always. Love is sharing."

"I didn't know that until I met you."

She raised herself up on her elbow and kissed him. He knew she meant the embrace to be a soft, caring one, but he'd been denied her for too long and lust reawakened in him.

"Are we done talking?" he asked.

"Why?"

He took her hand and guided it to his erection. "As long as I know you love me, everything will be fine."

Everything was fine. He made love to her all night and called in sick to work in the morning. He'd finally found the one woman he'd been searching for.

Epilogue

Their wedding day dawned bright and sunny. It seemed crazy but only three days had passed since she'd visited Joe's house and asked him to marry her. But he didn't want to wait another minute to start their life as man and wife.

Holly watched nervously from Joe's bedroom window as his family, her family and their friends gathered around the pool.

She'd have felt a lot better if her mom were with her today. But this morning her father had given her the rose-charm necklace that her mother had worn every day. She'd been so touched to have something of her mother's on her neck.

They'd asked Gina to be maid of honor, and Nick was standing up for Joe.

"Ready, Holly?" her dad asked from the doorway.

"Yes," she said, hurrying to his side.

She walked down the stairs and out onto the deck where Joe waited. He smiled at her and she felt her heart stop. She'd never expected love to feel like this. She'd never expected Mr. Right to look like him. She'd never dreamed happily-ever-after was in the cards for her.

But now she knew it was her destiny. The fate that Joe and she would make together.

She walked to him on a cloud of feeling and exchanged vows in a haze. The only part she was truly aware of was when he lowered his head to kiss her.

"You're mine," he said.

"And you are mine."

Their families and friends clapped and cheered. Holly was aware that she'd found the one man she'd spent her life searching for.... Well, maybe he'd found her.

*   *   *   *   *

DYNASTIES: THE BARONES

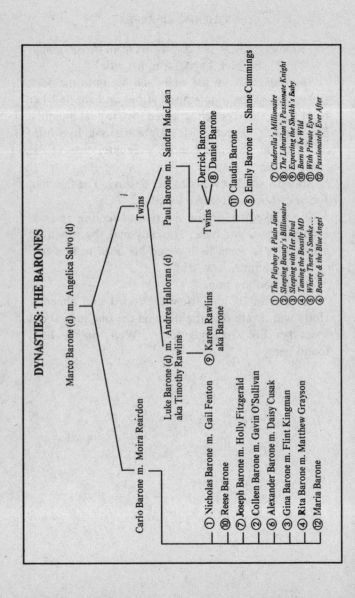

Marco Barone (d) m. Angelica Salvo (d)

Carlo Barone m. Moira Reardon

① Nicholas Barone m. Gail Fenton
⑩ Reese Barone
⑦ Joseph Barone m. Holly Fitzgerald
② Colleen Barone m. Gavin O'Sullivan
⑥ Alexander Barone m. Daisy Cusak
③ Gina Barone m. Flint Kingman
④ Rita Barone m. Matthew Grayson
⑫ Maria Barone

Twins

Luke Barone (d) m. Andrea Halloran (d)
aka Timothy Rawlins
⑨ Karen Rawlins
aka Barone

Paul Barone m. Sandra MacLean

Twins
Derrick Barone
⑧ Daniel Barone
⑪ Claudia Barone
⑤ Emily Barone m. Shane Cummings

① *The Playboy & Plain Jane*
② *Sleeping Beauty's Billionaire*
③ *Sleeping with Her Rival*
④ *Taming the Beastly MD*
⑤ *Where There's Smoke…*
⑥ *Beauty & the Blue Angel*
⑦ *Cinderella's Millionaire*
⑧ *The Librarian's Passionate Knight*
⑨ *Expecting the Sheikh's Baby*
⑩ *Born to be Wild*
⑪ *With Private Eyes*
⑫ *Passionately Ever After*

DYNASTIES: THE BARONES
continues...
Turn the page for a bonus look at
what's in store for you in the next
Barones book—only from
Silhouette Desire!

THE LIBRARIAN'S PASSIONATE
KNIGHT

by Cindy Gerard
August 2003

One

Daniel Barone wasn't sure why the woman had captured his attention. In the overall scheme of things, she was little more than a small speck of brown, virtually lost in the vibrant colors of Faneuil Hall Marketplace in the center of downtown Boston.

On this steamy August night, the open-air market was alive with colors and scents and sounds. She, quite literally, was not. Still, she'd drawn his undivided attention as he stood directly behind her at a pushcart outside the Quincy Market building.

Like a dozen or so others they were both waiting in line for ice cream. Unlike the others, who edged forward as placidly as milling cattle, she bounced with impatience. She just sort of danced in place, as

if she found irrepressible delight in the simple anticipation of getting her hands on an ice-cream cone.

For some reason it made Daniel smile. Her guile-
less exuberance charmed him, he supposed. And it
made him take time for a longer look.

She was average height—maybe a little on the
short side. Her hair wasn't quite blond, wasn't quite
brown, and there was nothing remotely sexy about
the short, pixieish cut. Her drab tan shorts and top
showed off a modest length of arm and leg and more
than adequately covered what could possibly be a
nice, tidy little body—who could tell? Other than the
wicked red polish splashed on her toenails there truly
wasn't a bright spot on the woman—until she turned
around with her much-awaited prize.

Behind owlish, black-rimmed glasses, a pair of
honey-brown eyes danced with anticipation, intelli-
gence and innate good humor. And when she took
that first long, indulgent lick, a smile of pure, decadent delight lit her ordinary face and transitioned un-
remarkable to breathtaking in a heartbeat. The watt-
age of that smile damn near blinded him.

"It was worth the wait," she murmured on a bliss-
ful sigh before she shouldered out of line and went
on about her business.

"And then some," Daniel agreed, and with a side-
long grin, watched the pleasant sway of her hips as
she walked away.

Wondering why a woman possessed of so much
vibrant and natural beauty would choose to hide it

behind professorial glasses, an unimaginative haircut and brown-paper-bag-plain clothes, he tracked her progress as she moved through the crowd. He was still watching when the kid wielding the ice-cream scoop nudged him back to the business at hand.

"Hey, Bud. You want ice cream or what?"

Daniel slowly turned his attention back to the counter. "Yeah. Sorry." He dug into his hip pocket for his wallet and, still grinning, hitched his chin in the general direction she'd taken. "I'll have what she had. Double dip."

The sweet, rich ice cream was a simple pleasure.

Like the unaffected smile of a pretty, satisfied woman.

He grinned again—this time in self-reproach— when he couldn't stop an image from forming.

Her head resting on his pillow…

Her body soft and warm and pliant beneath his…

Her incredible smile not only satisfied, but stunned, sated and spent…

* * * * *

Is your man too good to be true?

Hot, gorgeous AND romantic?
If so, he could be a Harlequin® Blaze™ series cover model!

Our grand-prize winners will receive a trip for two to New York City to shoot the cover of a Blaze novel, and will stay at the luxurious Plaza Hotel.

Plus, they'll receive $500 U.S. spending money!

The runner-up winners will receive $200 U.S. to spend on a romantic dinner for two.

It's easy to enter!

In 100 words or less, tell us what makes your boyfriend or spouse a true romantic and the perfect candidate for the cover of a Blaze novel, and include in your submission two photos of this potential cover model.

All entries must include the written submission of the contest entrant, two photographs of the model candidate and the Official Entry Form and Publicity Release forms completed in full and signed by both the model candidate and the contest entrant. Harlequin, along with the experts at Elite Model Management, will select a winner.

For photo and complete Contest details, please refer to the Official Rules on the next page. All entries will become the property of Harlequin Enterprises Ltd. and are not returnable.

Please visit www.blazecovermodel.com to download a copy of the Official Entry Form and Publicity Release Form or send a request to one of the addresses below.

Please mail your entry to: **Harlequin Blaze Cover Model Search**

In U.S.A.
P.O. Box 9069
Buffalo, NY
14269-9069

In Canada
P.O. Box 637
Fort Erie, ON
L2A 5X3

No purchase necessary. Contest open to Canadian and U.S. residents who are 18 and over.
Void where prohibited. Contest closes September 30, 2003.

HBCVRMODEL1

HARLEQUIN BLAZE COVER MODEL SEARCH CONTEST 3569 OFFICIAL RULES
NO PURCHASE NECESSARY TO ENTER

1. To enter, submit two (2) 4" x 6" photographs of a boyfriend or spouse (who must be 18 years of age or older) taken no later than three (3) months from the time of entry: a close-up, waist up, shirtless photograph; and a fully clothed, full-length photograph, then, tell us, in 100 words or fewer, why he should be a Harlequin Blaze cover model and how he is romantic. Your complete "entry" must include: (i) your essay, (ii) the Official Entry Form and Publicity Release Form printed below completed and signed by you (as "Entrant"), (iii) the photographs (with your hand-written name, address and phone number, and your model's name, address and phone number on the back of each photograph), and (iv) the Publicity Release Form and Photograph Representation Form printed below completed and signed by your model (as "Model"), and should be sent via first-class mail to either: Harlequin Blaze Cover Model Search Contest 3569, P.O. Box 9069, Buffalo, NY, 14269-9069, or Harlequin Blaze Cover Model Search Contest 3569, P.O. Box 637, Fort Erie, Ontario L2A 5X3. All submissions must be in English and be received no later than September 30, 2003. Limit: one entry per person, household or organization. **Purchase or acceptance of a product offer does not improve your chances of winning.** All entry requirements must be strictly adhered to for eligibility and to ensure fairness among entries.

2. Ten (10) Finalist submissions (photographs and essays) will be selected by a panel of judges consisting of members of the Harlequin editorial, marketing and public relations staff, as well as a representative from Elite Model Management (Toronto) Inc., based on the following criteria:

Aptness/Appropriateness of submitted photographs for a Harlequin Blaze cover—70%

Originality of Essay—20%

Sincerity of Essay—10%

In the event of a tie, duplicate finalists will be selected. The photographs submitted by finalists will be posted on the Harlequin website no later than November 15, 2003 (at www.blazecovermodel.com), and viewers may vote, in rank order, on their favorite(s) to assist in the panel of judges' final determination of the Grand Prize and Runner-up winning entries based on the above judging criteria. All decisions of the judges are final.

3. All entries become the property of Harlequin Enterprises Ltd. and none will be returned. Any entry may be used for future promotional purposes. Elite Model Management (Toronto) Inc. and/or its partners, subsidiaries and affiliates operating as "Elite Model Management" will have access to all entries including all personal information, and may contact any Entrant and/or Model in its sole discretion for their own business purposes. Harlequin and Elite Model Management (Toronto) Inc. are separate entities with no legal association or partnership whatsoever having no power to bind or obligate the other or create any expressed or implied obligation or responsibility on behalf of the other, such that Harlequin shall not be responsible in any way for any acts or omissions of Elite Model Management (Toronto) Inc. or its partners, subsidiaries and affiliates in connection with the Contest or otherwise and Elite Model Management shall not be responsible in any way for any acts or omissions of Harlequin or its partners, subsidiaries and affiliates in connection with the contest or otherwise.

4. All Entrants and Models must be residents of the U.S. or Canada, be 18 years of age or older, and have no prior criminal convictions. The contest is not open to any Model that is a professional model and/or actor in any capacity at the time of the entry. Contest void wherever prohibited by law; all applicable laws and regulations apply. Any litigation within the Province of Quebec regarding the conduct or organization of a publicity contest may be submitted to the Régie des alcools, des courses et des jeux for a ruling, and any litigation regarding the awarding of a prize may be submitted to the Régie only for the purpose of helping the parties reach a settlement. Employees and immediate family members of Harlequin Enterprises Ltd., D.L. Blair, Inc., Elite Model Management (Toronto) Inc. and their parents, affiliates, subsidiaries and all other agencies, entities and persons connected with the use, marketing or conduct of this Contest are not eligible to enter. Acceptance of any prize offered constitutes permission to use Entrants' and Models' names, essay submissions, photographs or other likenesses for the purposes of advertising, trade, publication and promotion on behalf of Harlequin Enterprises Ltd., its parent, affiliates, subsidiaries, assigns and other authorized entities involved in the judging and promotion of the contest without further compensation to any Entrant or Model, unless prohibited by law.

5. Finalists will be determined no later than October 30, 2003. Prize Winners will be determined no later than January 31, 2004. Grand Prize Winners (consisting of winning Entrant and Model) will be required to sign and return Affidavit of Eligibility/Release of Liability and Model Release forms within thirty (30) days of notification. Non-compliance with this requirement and within the specified time period will result in disqualification and an alternate will be selected. Any prize notification returned as undeliverable will result in the awarding of the prize to an alternate set of winners. All travelers (or parent/legal guardian of a minor) must execute the Affidavit of Eligibility/Release of Liability prior to ticketing and must possess required travel documents (e.g. valid photo ID) where applicable. Travel dates specified by Sponsor but no later than May 30, 2004.

6. Prizes: One (1) Grand Prize—the opportunity for the Model to appear on the cover of a paperback book from the Harlequin Blaze series, and a 3 day/2 night trip for two (Entrant and Model) to New York, NY for the photo shoot of Model which includes round-trip coach air transportation from the commercial airport nearest the winning Entrant's home to New York, NY, (or, in lieu of air transportation, $100 cash payable to Entrant and Model, if the winning Entrant's home is within 250 miles of New York, NY), hotel accommodations (double occupancy) at the Plaza Hotel and $500 cash spending money payable to Entrant and Model, (approximate prize value: $8,000), and one (1) Runner-up Prize of $200 cash payable to Entrant and Model for a romantic dinner for two (approximate prize value: $200). Prizes are valued in U.S. currency. Prizes consist of only those items listed as part of the prize. No substitution of prize(s) permitted by winners. All prizes are awarded jointly to the Entrant and Model of the winning entries, and are not severable - prizes and obligations may not be assigned or transferred. Any change to the Entrant and/or Model of the winning entries will result in disqualification and an alternate will be selected. Taxes on prize are the sole responsibility of winners. Any and all expenses and/or items not specifically described as part of the prize are the sole responsibility of winners. Harlequin Enterprises Ltd. and D.L. Blair, Inc., their parents, affiliates, and subsidiaries are not responsible for errors in printing of Contest entries and/or game pieces. No responsibility is assumed for lost, stolen, late, illegible, incomplete, inaccurate, non-delivered, postage due or misdirected mail or entries. In the event of printing or other errors which may result in unintended prize values or duplication of prizes, all affected game pieces or entries shall be null and void.

7. Winners will be notified by mail. For winners' list (available after March 31, 2004), send a self-addressed, stamped envelope to: Harlequin Blaze Cover Model Search Contest 3569 Winners, P.O. Box 4200, Blair, NE 68009-4200, or refer to the Harlequin website (at www.blazecovermodel.com).

Contest sponsored by Harlequin Enterprises Ltd., P.O. Box 9042, Buffalo, NY 14269-9042.

HBCVRMODEL2

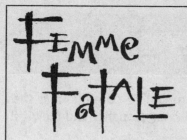

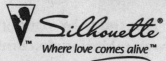

COMING NEXT MONTH

SDCNM0703